Flashes, Sparks, and Shorts

Flash One

Paul John Hausleben

Paul John Hausleben

Cover photograph, design, and cover concept by Paul John Hausleben

Rear cover photograph of the author is by Ms. Cali Rose

All other photographs and all drawings and images are by Paul John Hausleben

Published by God Bless the Keg Publishing LLC

Henrico, Virginia, U.S.A.

ISBN: 978-1-7330927-0-8

Dedication

To words. The ultimate power.

Flashes, Sparks, and Shorts

Flash One

Paul John Hausleben

Paul John Hausleben

Contents

Flashes, Sparks, and Shorts. Flash One

Paul John Hausleben

Somewhat of a Correct Answer . . . Pg. 278

Acknowledgements

Thank you to my friends and family and to the old man for his endless sayings and profound wisdom. Dad, your sayings go on forever. Herein, I only touched upon a few of them. Thank you, as always, to Harry M. Rogers Junior for his lifelong friendship and the glorious inspiration. Thank you to Lydia, Lopez, Harry, and many others for the suggestions of musical selections to use for inspirations for these stories. Thank you to all the talented music artists, songwriters and other creators for the words, the music and the inspiration to provide me with the basis for some of these stories.

"I have to write. It breathes life into my soul. Part of my very existence is to share parts and pieces of my soul with the world. It sustains me."

Paul John Hausleben

15 February 2021

Author Notes

About eight months prior to the writing of this collection, during the 2020 COVID-19 crisis and other assorted madness, I came across an article on writing flash fiction. It intrigued me because at that time, I was looking for a way to create some different material, but I was not willing to tear my soul out in a demanding project while doing so. Writing is very hard work. The world was topsy-turvy, and I had other demands upon myself while continuing to navigate through the daily madness.

When I stumbled upon the flash fiction information, I was between projects with two novels and a short story collection in the draft and in the preliminary editing phase. Additionally, I had some completed but unpublished material in the PJH story vault. I intended to use some material in the story vault for a series of short stories, consistent with a single theme of people returning home after long absences. When I originally completed the short story collections, I was not entirely happy about the theme and I delayed the publication of the material. The stories were acceptable, but they did not seem to fit into any niche within the many volumes of PJH publications. I often toss stories in the vault and revisit them later when a fresh idea wanders along.

In giving the stories in the story vault another glance or two and a careful reread, I decided the stories had some merit and I could use them as anchors in an eclectic collection that included the flash fiction. I could even keep the original theme intact, label them and, in doing so, hold open the door for a possible follow-up to this book. The idea and project took shape in my mind.

After reading the article and then reading the very loose and broad guidelines for writing flash fiction, I thought how that suited me rather well. There existed very few hard and fast rules for composition of such and what guidelines and rules exist for writing this fiction were rather broad. I have written a ton of material and I was searching for something very different to write and to have fun with a new project. This was a new project!

Of course, broad rules or not, I broke most of them, for writing flash fiction! In putting together this book, I categorized the work into three sections and named them accordingly.

I dug out and polished up some short stories hidden in the PJH vault, and those stories became the "Shorts." I wrote and compiled some quotes of life advice and wisdom; some humorous sayings and other words of drivel, and they became the "Sparks." The "Flashes" are the flash fiction pieces.

Some "Sparks" are my own thoughts and some of them; I borrowed from the endless wisdom of my old man. Regardless, the inspiration harkened me to my past as a dabbler in electrons and the title and the various words fell into my lap as "Flashes, Sparks, and Shorts."

Music is a huge part of my life and I always write with music in the background. In searching for inspiration for the flash fiction, as I often do and have done in the past, I used music as a source of themes for some flashes. My intention was to use the melodies, meanings and the lyrics as a basic theme for the stories and to get my creative juices flowing. My intention with the lyrics was not to plagiarize them, but to use them for the broad foundations of some stories. Other stories just jumped into my mind, or are the product of actual experiences that I have had in my life.

I feel it worked out rather well, and I enjoyed writing and creating the entire project.

I hope you can have some fun in trying to connect the dots of the various stories with the music, songs, and artists. Here are some musical artists, bands, and songwriters that provided inspiration for me in compiling these words:

Mark Knopfler OBE, solo and with Dire Straits.

David Gray.

Rick Wakeman.

YES.

Keane.

Jackson Browne.

The Sundays.

Martin Luther.

Gordon Lightfoot.

Lauren Diagle.

Johnny Cash.

Ian Anderson MBE, solo and with Jethro Tull.

Jennifer Thomas.

Wu-Tang Clan.

H.E.R.

Alan Jackson.

Coldplay and The Chainsmokers.

The Young Rascals.

America.

Bruce Springsteen.

Bryan Adams.

Jeff Lynne, solo and with the Electric Light Orchestra.

And a few others too!

Maybe you can even identify the individual songs and material that inspired some pieces.

I hope you enjoy reading these stories as much as I enjoyed writing them.

Thank you for reading them.

Paul John Hausleben

01 February 2021

Flash One

Through a Windowpane

She stood at the window for a long time and watched him as he left. He trudged down the street at a solemn pace. His struggling gait appeared as if his feet were too heavy to take the steps any faster than what he was doing.

It was raining. It was not a heavy rain, not a misty rain, but it was a moderate rain. The rain caused droplets of ill-fated cleansing to scurry down the glass of the window in front of her. An annoying rain. A gloomy rain that despite the lateness of the morning hour caused the streetlights to linger in their glow. The traffic light at the corner cast a beautiful red color on the wet street. It caught her eye when it changed from red to green. She thought how the red color was prettier.

A truck rumbled by on the city street and the glass windowpane shook a little in front of her and in a strange reaction to the vibration of the glass, she reached out and gently placed her fingers upon the glass to stop the shaking. She wanted no more noises than necessary right now. Her mind required quiet.

He disappeared from her view. Around the corner. Into the grit of the city. Into the glow of the streetlights.

With a deep sigh, she thought, 'He is gone

forever now. Just a memory.'

The apartment they shared for these past few years was nothing special. Kind of dark, kind of dingy, somewhat solemn, and today it was gloomy. Then again, in rethinking that description, as of late, it was always gloomy. It wasn't always that way. A few years ago, they were happy. Nowadays, not so much. In her heart, she knew the betrayal of their love always lay in some dark corner of their life, just waiting to jump out and snatch both of them by their hearts. Last night it did so. Yet as she watched the rain run down the glass and the city traffic roll by in front of her, she felt very little sadness. In fact, if she examined her soul carefully and openly, she felt some relief. Relief in that it was time to move on in her life, in his life, and that despite the gloom there was always a reason that things happen as they do so.

The city bus rolled to a stop in front of her. The number eighteen bus. It stopped at the corner. One person got off, and no one jumped on to it. The bus stopped there and idled. As it did so many times per day.

'How many times?' she thought. 'Many.' She never really paid much attention to how many times it stopped there. Now that it was all over, she could jump on that bus and go anywhere. Literally, anywhere. What did it matter? It didn't. One road, one bus, could lead to another road, to another bus, or to a train or to a plane or to wherever. To a new life. That is what she needed to do. To take the next step on the road to wherever. She had the money, she had the time, and now, she had the peace in her soul to do it. He could have the apartment, the furniture, the memories; he could have everything. His new lover could share the same bed that they shared. Because she really didn't care. All she would do is pack a suitcase, grab some important papers, her credit cards, some cash, her cell phone and her heart and she would disappear. No way would she leave her heart here. That had to go with her.

The bus pulled away, and she vowed that the next time it arrived she would be on it. Once more, she reached up and ran her fingers along the glass. She turned away and for a fleeting second, she thought about how she wished it could be different somehow.

She thought, 'It is amazing what you can see if you glance long enough and hard enough through a windowpane. Pretty colors, gloom, rain remnants, lights aglow, a bus, a gritty city and a vision for a new life. Through a windowpane.'

Her heart jumped when there was a gentle knock upon the front door.

The knock echoed with repentance.

Flash Two

Roundabout

The roundabout was his most lucrative location. On the grass near the edge of the curb where he could advocate to the drivers of the vehicles heading northbound. Southbound drivers were cheap. He never could figure that out.

He preferred the title of "Homeless Advocator" as opposed to a "Homeless Beggar." He advocated for funds. Begging had such demeaning implications.

He had heard that there were not too many roundabouts left in this country. This one in northern New Jersey was legendary. He heard Massachusetts had many of them too. He had never been there, and the way things were going; it looked as if he never would. Someday, he would like to go there. See Fenway Park. His family was enormous Yankee fans, and Yankee Stadium was very cool. What he recalled of it, at least.

It was rainy and cold and in late October. Other than Christmastime of the year and snowy days, rainy and cold days were his most rewarding. On these days, it was difficult to roll out of the warmth of the homeless shelter's bed, even if the place was an inner-city dump. How he wished it would receive enough funds to repair all the issues, freshen it up, fix the plumbing, put in new floors, but that was not happening. They barely had enough volunteers to staff the shifts and enough funds to buy the food these days. It seems as if they always come up short from a lack of donations in order to prepare enough meals and keep the heat on during the cold months.

Someday sufficient funds would arrive.

Perhaps.

Yesterday was a Monday. It was an awful day. Everyone is angry on Mondays. To compound the misery; it was beautiful weather. The sun was out, and the sky was clear. No one had sympathy, and even the regulars sped by him without nary a coin or even a wave or a donut or a cup of coffee or a bottle of water. Sunny days sucked. He could have also done without the jerk tossing a cup of coffee on him when he turned his back.

A toss, laced with the usual, "Get a job, ya lazy jackass!"

If he could; he would. A long time ago, he had a good job, a trade, a family, and even a house. A long time ago, until fate and circumstances stole it from him and gave him a limp and an arm that never healed. The company paid out; or so they claimed.

At least the coffee was cold. Last time it was hot.

Now it was Tuesday with a fresh start and a rain-soaked day full of sympathy, and the Homeless Advocator wandered up and down the grass, waving his new sign. He made it with some help from the kitchen staff at the homeless shelter. They used a fresh piece of cardboard ripped from a box of carrots donated by the food wholesalers. They wrote his words of inspiration for the day on the box with a wax crayon that the staff used to write on boxes they stored in the freezer. The wax did not run in the moisture. One side of the sign loudly displayed "Carrots" with a colored-ink imprint of a bunch of carrots. The other side had his message for the day.

A message inspired by the hot coffee toss.

'When a person offends you, why not give them a piece of your heart instead of a piece of your mind?'

So far, his little piece of literary inspiration was working rather well. Many thumbs up. Along with ten dollars in bills, about eight bucks in coins, a warm cup of coffee (handed, not tossed) a few bottles of water and an umbrella. All before ten in the morning. He had four umbrellas already. All of them kept stashed in his secret locker at the home's shelter, but he welcomed another one. He could sell it for fifty cents, or maybe even a buck. He never used umbrellas during his advocating sessions. It invoked sympathy and kept the donations down. It is better for the rain to soak you to the bones.

The man drove a fancy SUV. It looked brand new. Had to cost a pretty penny. Four-wheel-drive and all the whistles and bells. It had a metallic black finish, the rain highlighted rather well. Special wheels and he could hear the music playing as the driver rolled to a stop right in front of where he stood, holding his sign that was getting progressively wetter. The message began to run. Despite the wax crayon used in its creation. The message would not last too much longer, and then it would fade from the cardboard and the minds of those who already read it.

He held the sign up higher and zeroed in as the traffic of the commute slowed and forced the SUV to a stop. The technique was perfect and honed over many years of practice. The driver was affluent and did not want to face the hardships of life staring at him from out the side of his vision. The driver felt the burn and the pain and he tried very hard not to make eye contact while most likely praying for the traffic to move once more. The sign wiggled, and the holder walked a little closer until finally, the driver after making believe he was fiddling with his defroster controls, hit the window button on the driver's side window and the window gracefully glided down. A handsome face appeared from behind the glass, and the man reached for something from inside the vehicle and handed it to the Homeless Advocator.

"Here," the driver said, "it is all that I have. I hope it gets you a few bucks. I always lose, anyway. Gonna give up wasting my money on 'em. By the way . . . nice sign."

With those words, the window went up, the traffic cleared, and the driver effortlessly navigated the SUV around the rest of the roundabout. The Homeless Advocator stared down at the lottery ticket in his hands and with a shrug of his shoulders; he stuffed it into his pants pocket. Front pocket. Right side. He then walked to the other side of the roundabout.

'Let's see how cheap the southbound crowd is today,' he thought.

The rain came down harder.

The new floors of the homeless shelter were the best of the best. Durable vinyl. Easy to clean.

"Should last fifty years," the flooring sales associate told him.

New appliances, new beds, all fresh paint—three coats, all new plumbing. And a new roof. The facility maintenance man said the roof was on its last legs.

He always loved the Jersey Shore. Growing up, his old man always took them to the shore for a few days. They did not have much, but the old man did the best that he could back then. His front porch faced west. He picked a small house on the inlet because he loved to sit on a porch and watch the sunsets. The colors fascinated him.

Spark One

All about Trust

"When someone keeps telling you to trust them; don't trust them."

Flash Three

Around Eight O'clock

It was Saturday morning, around eight o'clock. He knew that his girlfriend's father was off to work already. He worked every Saturday and Wednesday was his day off.

The summer was almost over. You could feel the change of the seasons in the air. Especially so in the early morning. When the dew sets hard. When the moisture invades the grass all the way down to the roots where the plants touch the soil.

He could see his warm breath hit the air in puffs. Gentle puffs while he wiped the dew off his prized Camaro. The car of his dreams, preparing to ride to change his life and her life and ride off to God only knows with the woman of his dreams. Perhaps.

The air temperature would warm up later, maybe by the time they hit Interstate Eighty. They could roll down the windows. Perhaps.

All the clothes he owned and the few possessions that he claimed in his entire life of twenty-three years sat in the trunk of the Camaro. The clothes fit in one small bag and the possessions hardly took up half the trunk. In his wallet, he had his life savings. One-thousand-twenty-seven dollars. Along with pocket change. His one suit, as his dear mother called it, "His Sunday or Funeral suit" hung on a hanger in the back seat. On the hook. If his gal agreed to his plan, there was more than enough room for her clothes and belongings.

Women usually had more clothes and belongings than men did.

When he tossed the wiping rag into the trunk and slammed the lid down, he thought, 'Hell, anyone had more stuff than I do.'

That fact did not bother him in the least. In fact, it made it much easier for this plan to take place.

He climbed into the Camaro, fired off the LT1, and the engine roared to life with a deep power that always set his blood flowing throughout his entire body. Just as she did when she smiled at him and when they made love. Other men would look at his gal and think that she was not a bombshell, but to him she was the entire universe. He loved the way her hair fell all around him when they locked in an embrace, and the way sweat appeared on her upper lips when they loved so deep and so powerfully. The flash of her dark eyes followed by a sigh and a smile.

The clutch hit the floor, and the gearshift set hard into first gear after a quick jaunt in reverse. He stopped in the turnaround and stared at the house. His uncle and aunt were good people. The best. They took him in when his parents left this world, and he owed them a huge debt of gratitude. His uncle understood the need to leave; however, his aunt not so much. The discussion last night was difficult. He would miss them, and his cousins were very cool.

Christmas and Thanksgiving were for visiting.

The tires spun, and the engine roared. He heard and felt some rocks kick up from under the tires.

He knew his aunt was behind the curtain peaking out at the scene with tears in her eyes and his uncle had his hand on her back in support and comfort. That was the kind of love he wished for with his woman and damn well, if he was not off to claim it.

There was nothing left here for him. For them. It was a tired old Jersey Shore town. Old and tired.

It was a short drive to her house. They grew up together in this little Jersey Shore town. Fell in love in the third grade.

The Camaro spun its tires again when he hit the edge of his girlfriend's driveway. Every time, he downshifted and then popped the clutch a little. LT1 power. Old-school Detroit. He was sure the roar of the engine alerted everyone in his woman's house that he arrived. This visit was unscheduled. No one knew he was coming over today. Not this early. Not even his girlfriend. Especially not her.

There she was on the porch, her dress wisped around her ankles. The sun shone all around her body and he smiled and held his breath as he pushed in the clutch, shifted to first gear and quieted the roar of the LT1. Then he moved the ignition key to the accessory position, pushed in the tape, dialed up the song and turned up the volume. His woman stood with her hands on her hips and shrugged her shoulders.

"Do Ya? Do ya? Do, ya, do ya, want my love?" Jeff sang one of their favorite songs as he jumped out of the Camera and without saying a word; he ran to the trunk, used his trunk key and popped it open. He pulled out the bag, held it in the air, and smiled as Jeff continued to ask the same question with that mean-ass guitar lick.

Now, she grew concerned as she realized their dreams were suddenly reality before her eyes. Those dreamy discussions after making love in the back seat of the Camaro were no longer so dreamy.

Her mother appeared on the porch. She held the screen door gently open, and then she carefully let it close without a noise. His brother must still be sleeping. Her mother wiped her hands on the dishtowel she held in her hands and then tucked it into her apron. Concern washed over her face as she realized the situation.

His throat closed; he did not waver in holding the bag in the air.

He thought, 'Now or never, baby.'

Yet, he spoke not a single word. Some scenes in life require no words. His gal only stood and studied him for what was only seconds or perhaps a minute, but seemed as if it were ten lifetimes. Or more.

Suddenly, she turned and spun on her heels. Once more, her dress wisped at her ankles and she pulled the door open and darted inside the house. Her mother glanced quickly in his direction; their eyes met briefly, before spinning on her heels and following her daughter into the home. This time no one held open the door. If he had to bet, her brother was now awake.

Slowly, he lowered the bag and held it at his side as he peered at the porch. His throat remained closed and even a swallow did not clear it. He thought this would be easier with her father gone and at work. Perhaps.

Lives in the balance.

"Where are we going?" She asked as she rolled

down the window and the wind from Interstate 80 rushed in and blew her hair all around her face. She pushed her hair away from in front of her face as she turned to face him and study him, as he remained focused down the road.

"Somewhere out there," he said while waving with one hand at the windshield. "We will let our hearts tell us when to stop. I mean, does it really matter?"

"No, no," she shook her head and smiled while staring out the window and pushing her hair away again from her face, "not really. As long as we are together. That is all that really matters."

It was Saturday morning. Around eleven o'clock now.

The LT1 purred like a kitten.

Flash Four

Her Jeans Were Tight Now

Her jeans were tight now.

She pulled them on and wiggled a bit, sucked in hard and then worked the button on the waist closed.

'It is more that I just washed them rather than the fact I have gained weight,' she thought.

She remained partly convinced that was true. When in doubt, always accuse the laundry shrinkage as the culprit for the tight waist.

She wiggled a bit more, squatted down in an effort to loosen them, and tugged at the legs to encourage a bit of a stretch in the newly washed jeans. In front of the mirror, she checked out her backside and spun around and in a wave of self-examination; she thought she looked rather sexy. A new blouse easily slipped over her; it was on sale yesterday. A v-neck to reveal just a whisper of modest cleavage. The blouse was light and airy, with a touch of frill along the sleeves, intensely black in color, and she loved it. Black jeans, black blouse, and a pair of black dress boots with an illusion of a high-heel.

She also knew that all he wore was black.

Always.

Supposition mixed with evidence to lead her to

the belief that black was his thing. A new haircut, not too short, but the stylist convinced her to go trendy and allow a touch of a wave of hair to cross her face.

"If you do not want to do the sexy stare through the wave of hair, tuck it behind your ear. Make sure that you highlight your eyes and lashes with liner and stare out at him. You're gonna melt this dude," was the stylist's advice.

She went with it and she dyed her hair a shade or two off her natural color, because there was a hint of gray along the edges and here and there. The finishing touches were her grandmother's heirloom hoop earrings, and the matching single gold chain of a necklace that she just had to wear. They were not expensive pieces; they were slightly tarnished pieces of gold, with some waves of mystery involved in them. She was very close to Grammy, and she missed her every day. Through hints, parts, and pieces of conversation, she was sure that a special lover gave the pieces to her grandmother. Maybe before Grandpa was in the picture, or maybe not. Just the manner in which Grammy held them in her hands and stared at them with this love-struck look in her eyes made her sure that she was correct in her assumption. He must have been the love of her life, and these were precious reminders. Grammy left them to her in her will because Grammy knew that her granddaughter knew the true history of the pieces. Now, they were going to bring her luck today with the unapproachable man in black.

Every Sunday he was there for brunch.

Today was Sunday.

He would be there today. At the end of the bar,

sitting alone, nursing a beer, chatting occasionally with the bartender, or a server than he seemed to know for a long time, but mostly remaining silent and pensive. Always dressed in black, perfect in his features, stunning in appearance. She had never seen a more handsome man than he was. At a guess, he was at least ten years older than she was . . . he was one of those lucky people that it was impossible to tell how old he was. Their age meant nothing. She couldn't care less. Her heart would go pitter-patter at the sight of him. They had only very scant bits of conversation in the past. She would always say something stupid and irrelevant. He would smile, comment and say a few polite words with his hard New Jersey accent and then he would fade away. As soon as she tried to break the ice, it would freeze over once more.

From milking information from the bartender who was a gal she trusted and knew (and who, despite best efforts, had no success in her own pursuit of the same man) for a long time, he loved music . . . primarily classic rock-and-roll. He was a fan of ice hockey too. His server friend coughed up that tidbit. Other than those subjects, the inside scoop well ran dry. He never spoke of much else other than general subjects. No one even knew what he did for a living. However, she knew that his favorite band was the Electric Light Orchestra. Hockey was a sport that she would not tackle, but she could handle music. She was now the proud owner of every recording that ELO ever created, thought about, or laid down on CD, tape, or vinyl, and she had to admit that the music was very cool. Even if this day was a flop, at least she had a new favorite band. She knew every song, every album release and every detail of the band, and her cell phone had every MP3 recoding of ELO loaded on it now. She even knew the name of the street in Birmingham, England, where Jeff Lynne grew up. The encyclopedia-like knowledge of ELO would be the icebreaker. After all, she had some English blood in her veins.

She was no English Rose, but today was the day.

A short drive in her car, a final check of her makeup, a confident walk into the restaurant and an adjustment to the light inside as opposed to the outside light. There he was at the bar in his favorite bar stool, and today, he was looking better than the laws of human attraction should allow. Faint be her heart because the gods smiled upon her . . . the seat next to him was open.

"Hi, is this seat taken?" Her question floated in the air while she allowed the dangle of hair across her face. Her enchanting eyes flickered while asking the question. He finished a sip of his beer, smiled that killer smile, and his golden voice riveted her soul.

With a wave in the direction of the bar stool, the words floated in the air, "No. Please. Sit. Enjoy."

She swore that out of the corner of his eyes, he watched her settle into the bar stool and there were smiles all around.

Damn, she wished that her jeans were not so tight.

The bartender smiled with a rather phony smile laced with a touch of jealousy and greeted her, and the bartender's smile told the story that she knew the plan.

The bartender winked, nodded, and took her drink order. She looked down as her cell phone blinked and beeped with a text.

It was a text from the bartender and it read, **"Good luck. I never have had any. May the best girl win."**

Two Mimosas later and the silence remained. He had not said another word and her palms were sweaty and she was feeling a little loose and loopy. Time to make a move. Time for a third Mimosa. A girl needs her courage. Liquid or otherwise.

Today was the day. Convinced that small talk would not cut it, she went for the brass ring. She opened her purse, pulled out her earbuds and placed them in her ears. God gave her a gift, and that was her singing voice. Well, God also gave her some very nice female curves, a pretty face and other attributes, but to this man, she was sure that meant little. When you looked like he did, women threw those gifts at him right and left.

With a flick of the screen, she dialed up *Out of the Blue*, scrolled to *It's Over* and waltzed in for the kill. While pretending to glance at the menus to pick out some food, in order to absorb the alcohol taking over her mind and body, off she went into the opening words.

Not a loud singing voice, not an obnoxious singing voice, but just loud enough, "Summer came and passed away. . .." His head swung around and he smiled.

Pay dirt smelled so sweet. As if, it was fresh-turned dirt in a spring garden.

"It's over, it's over. . .."

Another smile and some words as he stared at her.

"Electric Light Orchestra, huh? I would not think they were your style," He said with a knockout smile and a wave of his hands. It took all that she could muster up to pretend that she was only slightly paying attention.

While taking the earbuds out of her ears, she asked, "Say again. I did not hear you. I am sorry."

"No, my apologies for bothering you. I said, ELO. I did not figure you to be an ELO type of woman. I am a huge fan of ELO. Huge."

"Oh, cool. That is a coincidence. I love them too," she said with one of the best acting jobs this side of Hollywood.

He paused and then waved at her with her hand. It had to be a New Jersey thing. She found it very appealing.

"I have seen you in here before . . . but there is something different. Maybe your hair?"

"Well, yes, it is a new style. I was not too sure about it. And yes, I love ELO. Out of the Blue is amazing."

Once more, he studied her and her heart went pitter-patter and boom, boom, and a final, resounding BOOM! He gently reached up, pushed the dangle of hair out of her face, and tucked it gently behind her ear.

"I needed to move that hair to see your face better. You are stunning, please, be sure about it. You look gorgeous. Say, let me buy your drinks there. And lunch too."

The words were almost a sputter, "Well, okay. Thank you. . .."

"What is your favorite ELO song? I am kind of

partial to, It's Over, and appears if you are too."

Two hours later, he had invited her to an Electric Light Orchestra reunion concert in Philadelphia, scheduled for about two months from now. Two months! Oh my! He said that he had extra tickets. She missed the Philadelphia date in her research, and she honestly had no idea they were even touring again. Wow, thank you, God! Oh yes, and he invited her to dinner for later that evening. He paid their tabs; they slipped off the bar stools and headed for the door together.

Yes, today was the day.

Her cell phone blinked and beeped and with a smile, she looked over at the bartender who had sent a simple text, **"Wow! How did u pull that off?!!!**

She paused and texted back, **"I had a secret weapon. Mr. Blue Sky. Google it."**

Yes, her jeans were tight now.

Yet, she had a feeling that in a little while they were going to become much looser.

Flash Five

A Gift. Freely Given

On the first day, the drill instructor told us that some of us might die. It was a risk that I knew I needed to accept. Honestly, I never thought it would happen to me. I never really did.

I was wrong.

One of my brothers in arms holds my hand. Tightly. He tells me to hang on. He tugs at my body armor. I cannot really see him. Everything is a blur.

There is no pain. There was for a second, but now it is gone.

A Navy Corpsman works on me. He shouts something. It is hopeless. I feel my life fading.

It will be all right. I knew the risk. I signed up for this. I am a volunteer.

The sun fades. I see my lover. I see her lovely face. I feel our passion. I see our daughter. I will never see her grow up. I will never see her laugh, smile, or dance.

I see my mother, my father, and my sister. My best friend. They will cry. They will miss me. They will stand by and weep as they lower me into the cold ground. They will fly the American flag from their porches.

It will fly free and it will fly proud.

It will be all right. I knew the risk. I never thought it would happen to me. I was wrong. Some Marines must pay the price. There have been many before me and there will be many after me. Those who are willing. Where others choose to hide and to pretend.

Damn, I am only twenty-two years old. That is how it goes. I did this for you. And for him and for her and for them. I don't even know your names. I never will. Please never waste this effort. This life.

I gave you this gift, and it was free. It is my life. My commitment to you and yours. So that you could live, free. To do as you please. As you choose to do.

I knew the risk. No one made me sign up for this. Everyone must die. My time is now here.

Remember.

Yet, as I lay dying and bleeding—I only wish for one thing. That you know that I did this for you and yours and for them. I did this, not for any specific skin color, or a man, or a woman, or for any race, or for any religion.

For you.

It is a gift. Freely given.

It is my life.

Spark Two

Actors and Such

"All the actors ain't in Hollywood."

Flash Six

When You Love a Writer

They had been best friends for years.

She tilted her head and smiled, and then she slowly retreated and leaned back into the park bench. The waning sunlight danced in her eyes. He studied the light, and pure magic ensued.

She smiled once more. He studied her full lips. He longed to taste her, and she knew it. Perhaps, for her, it was the influence of the wine, or for him, it was the influence of the Manhattans they enjoyed at dinner. Manhattans laced with Irish. A different choice for him on this go-around. He usually picked bourbon. This time he chose Irish whiskey.

They had come to the park to walk around and sober up. A bit.

Perhaps it was the drink. Perhaps not.

The longing was mutual. It had been forever. Maybe even longer.

Once again, she tilted her head and the distance between them closed, and finally, they kissed.

At first, it was awkward. First kisses often are, even between soulmates. After all, it is a first kiss that waited from the dawn of time to occur. Their front teeth might have clunked together. After an awkward beginning, their obvious bond and love overcame them both, and the kiss deepened. It grew and grew in intensity until it arrived in a climax of passion. A dance of tongues. She could taste the whiskey. He could taste the wine. She moaned in his mouth and pushed her fingers into his hair. He did the same.

Breathless, their lips left each other. Her soul told her to vow that would be their first kiss, but not their last. He leaned forward while she studied his face. Her courage grew as they gently touched their foreheads together. She swore she could feel his heartbeat through the touch.

"I am in love with you. I have been . . . forever."

Her admittance came without reluctance. Uninhibited.

His answer remained laced in brutal honesty. It was the only way that he knew how to deliver them because he, too, loved her. Forever. If they were going to be lovers, then honesty was paramount. Above reproach.

His words came out of his mouth as if they were a whisper. Gentle, quiet, yet all consuming.

"I am a writer. Do you understand what you are getting into when you say that you are in love with a writer? Because I will never be anything but a writer. What you are signing up for in this world of words and madness?"

She studied his mouth as he spoke the words and nodded her head.

"Okay . . . I will never recall your birthday or our wedding anniversary, or our children's birthdays . . . but I will always recall what you are wearing today, how your lips taste, how you moaned when our lips met for the first time and how the sunlight is reflecting the highlights of your hair. Right now."

Another nod.

"I will need my alone time to write but I will never shut you out, but if this makes some sense, during those writing times . . . I will shut you out. I will only hear half of what you say but will absorb all of your words. You will appear in a million words and in every sentence, but you might not recognize your own being or even a semblance of yourself. I will create characters that are similar to you and some who compete with you for my affection. Let's not venture into any jealousy because your competition is purely fictional. I will walk around in a daze as I figure and work out simple and complex story lines, and I will never hear a word that you say. Yet, I will fully embrace every word that you speak."

Another nod.

"We will live hand-to-mouth. This will never be an easy life. Yet . . . I have to write. It breathes life into my soul. Part of my very existence is to share parts and pieces of my soul with the world. It sustains me. I will have to tend bar to make ends meet and you will need to wait tables and we will never have enough money."

Another nod.

"I will forever dream of writing the great novel, of making the best seller's list and hitting the perfect chord of words that will make me a reader's dream and a household name, but chances are, I might never make it there and we will forever dwell on the precipices of the perfect collection of words. There will never be anything tangible. It will forever be some random smattering of words, the dreams of a poet, the ramblings of a wordsmith, and of a writer. You will lead that life . . . if you choose to love . . .

a writer. It will not be romantic. Yet, I can guarantee you will experience passion that knows no boundaries. I will describe every inch of your glorious body in words, for all the readers to share and immerse themselves in your beauty and in our private life and our own secrets. Readers will feel our pain, our love, our happiness and our sadness. It will be moody. It will be anything but private. I might forget your name and call you by a character's name."

Another nod. Followed by a wide smile that melted his heart. He leaned back and studied her beautiful face.

"Yet, please, let me emphasize and always remember that I will never forget this day, or how you smell right now or how the sunlight always reflects the highlights the different layers of hues in your hair and what type of nail polish that you wear right now, or how soft your skin is, or how glorious it will be to make love to you for the first time. This memory and this truth will someday, make a very glorious story. I too, love you and I have forever and I will forever be yours."

This time, no nod. Determination crossed her face.

Her resulting words reflected and emphasized the same determination.

"Are you finished with your words? Are you finished with your stern warnings and disclaimers? Are you done with your ramblings?" She asked.

This time, he nodded.

"Then tell me where to sign up and before you speak another word . . . kiss me until my toes curl because I love you . . . writer and all the baggage that goes with you and all that other bullshit. Just shut up and kiss me. Writer."

They kissed and their toes curled.

Together. In unison.

They had been best friends for years.

Now, they were lovers.

Forever.

Flash Seven

Tougher Than the Rest

It was January and the after-the-holidays-doldrums settled in. So did the deep freeze and the snow and ice and cold.

The old gin joint was dusty. Very dusty. Dimly lit, too. It was a gin joint in Hawthorne, New Jersey. The neon sign hanging from the front post of the building on the east corner of the porch needed repair. Some letters in the sign did not light. The interior of the gin joint was dusty. Dark wood reflected what little light there was inside. A jukebox glowed brighter than anything else, along with a tired old sign of beer nostalgia.

It smelled like stale beer.

The Front Porch was the name of the joint. It sat on an old and tired street corner on Wagaraw Road in Hawthorne, New Jersey.

The Front Porch sponsored a program called, "The 100 Beer Club."

The beer loving patrons sampled various beers and when they did so, each beer drinker received special badges to wear. It was old Harry's idea, and it was a grand idea. He had created a marketing niche. Harry owned the gin joint for thirty-five years. Old Harry was gone now. Six months ago, on this very day. Harry was a legend around these parts. A tough guy—war veteran. He told great stories of combat lore.

His son-in-law took over the business.

Yet, Harry lingered in the dusty corners and within the dim lights. This little enclave of beer and cocktail lovers missed Harry, but somehow, Harry tried very hard to tell them that he was still here.

His ghost remained.

The young man knew the 100 Beer Club was a gimmick to entice you to drink more beers and try odd and unusual beers, nevertheless, he enjoyed the experience. Since old Harry was gone now, he hoped that his son-in-law kept the 100 Beer Club active. He thought that it was very cool. Besides, the ice-cold sampling mugs of the beers were only thirty cents each. He wore each badge with pride and occasionally, someone would notice them and strike up a conversation. If it was a beautiful young woman who pointed at the badge and asked about it, then it was even better. If not, then conversation was conversation.

It was a snowy day and the young man had spent the best part of the day in a snowplow truck and outside in the ice, wind and snow while clearing, shoveling and pushing snow, but now, the storm ended and it was time to relax. The young man worked in building maintenance for a large corporation that owned and operated several properties in the northern New Jersey area. When it snowed, it translated to job security and overtime pay. Overtime paychecks meant that there were a few bucks more in the young man's wallet. He was only twenty-three years of age and he had the world by the horns.

On the other hand, he had the world by another description.

Yet, when you are so very young, there are many lessons to learn. To earn. To live and to experience.

It was the young man's plan to come into The Front Porch and he would enjoy a few beers, knock some ice and snow off the plow, head home, sleep, and relax. Tomorrow, the young man and his fellow crew would spread salt and touch up the edges. It was a long day for him; he had been working since three in the morning, but his father taught him that with hard work there would eventually be great rewards.

His father told him that he needed to be, "Tougher than the rest."

The young man took the words and advice to heart. His old man was a working man too, and he was a brilliant man with immeasurable street smarts.

It will be a cold night and the freeze will set in. Tomorrow would be no joke. Right now, it was time to unwind. Harry would understand. That was part of his vision and mission too.

The bar was quiet and mostly empty. Except for the ghost of Harry and an elderly man who held down the last barstool on the right-hand side of the bar. The young man spotted him sitting there and made note of his presence. It was the elderly man's usual spot. It seemed as if he was always there. The young man noted the fact that the elderly man turned and faced him as he walked into the bar. That in itself was unusual behavior because, generally, the elderly man never even noticed him . . . or anyone else.

Except, maybe, for Harry.

Apparently, the snowstorm kept most people away. However, neither the elderly man nor the young man stayed away. They seemed cut as if they cut them both from the same mold. They were many years apart in age; however, there was little doubt they were from the same mold.

To the young man's surprise, the elderly man patted the barstool next to him and invited me to sit next to him. The young man nodded and accepted the invitation.

The bartender looked up; he, too, seemed shocked at the elderly man's unusual invitation, and upon seeing the young man, he knew the patron's favorite pour, and he leaned into one. The young man greeted the elderly man as he settled onto the stool. No sampling today.

No badges required. Not today.

A regular pour.

"Only one dollar today," the bartender said with a point at the regular-sized mug. "A reward for even coming in," he added with a smile as he handed off the mug to the young man.

"How ya doin'?" the elderly man asked in a Hawthorne, New Jersey accent. His eyes checked out the winter-reddened face of the young man, his wool-lined vest with work gloves stuffed in the pockets, and an ice-caked watchman's cap jammed down on his head.

"Nice to see a young workin' man, workin'. Most guys ya age are home sleepin' watchin' bullshit on TV. Lazy asses. Ya not. Ya, a hard-workin' guy. Seen ya in here often. Sluggin' it out every day. So ya been out plowin' and shovelin' snow all day?

Long day, huh?"

"Yes, sir. Been out since three in the morning," the young man answered in a Paterson, New Jersey accent while he picked up the mug to enjoy his reward. After a long glorious sip and with just a hint of a smile upon his face, which the elderly man nodded at in approval, the young man placed the mug upon the coaster and said, "Wow. That first taste is always amazing." He smacked his lips and then asked, "I guess the snow did not keep you in the house, huh?"

The elderly man's eyes widened while a deep sigh emitted from him.

He leaned into his beer and then after a taste and replacing the beer mug on the bar counter, he lifted his eyes and glanced at the old cloth patch stapled to the wood near the cash register behind the bar counter. The United States Army Airborne insignia graced the patch. The patch was dusty but proud.

Old Harry was airborne. A Ranger.

The elderly man kept his eyes on the patch while he spoke just above a whisper, "Kid, I stormed the beach on D-Day. Old Harry was there too. Different beach. There were shells, explosions, and bullets flying all around. I made it. Many of my friends did not. Harry made it too. I damn sure ain't gonna let a little twelve-inch snowstorm stop me from enjoying a few cold beers. Yeah, man, I gotta admit that those first sips are amazin'."

After speaking, the elderly man smiled and lifted his mug and the young man did the same.

Tougher than the rest.

Both of them.

Harry, too.

We need to be so now and forever.

Flash Eight

Echoes within the Stillness

The house was quiet and still, yet; there were echoes within the stillness.

It was late on a Saturday afternoon. Just before six o'clock. His usual dinner hour. Their usual dinner hour.

The old man took a deep breath, placed his hands on the wooden arms of his old easy chair, pushed off with a loud groan and he painfully and slowly stood up. He carefully shifted his feet to measure his balance and picked each foot up to gain control of his stance.

To think how many of the simple things in life we take for granted. Then, we grow old and everything is difficult.

He thought, 'Nothing is easy now.'

His eyes glanced at the easy chair next to his as he squinted at the details. He moved his feet a few steps in the chair's direction, then leaned forward to hold on to the wooden table centered between them.

'Steady now,' were his thoughts and once grounded, he moved again in the chair's direction. He reached up and ran his hand along the wooden arms of the chair.

The chair was empty.

With a gentle pat on the arm of the chair, he turned and slowly shuffled off in the kitchen's direction. On the way, he stopped and grabbed two sweaters for the hallway closet. His and hers.

It took the old man and his old legs what seemed as if it was a lifetime to make it to the kitchen. Where the second hand of the old clock on the wall kept time with a halting second hand. An audible click measured the seconds. Of a lifetime of audible clicks. More echoes with the stillness.

First, he lovingly draped her sweater over the back of one chair and he put his sweater on. Then he moved the candle to the center of the table and lit the wick. With a flash and a spark along with a whisper of smoke, a gentle light broadcasted on the old wallpaper on the walls above the table. The wallpaper that his wife picked out. Some of the seams peeled now. Six months ago, he used some glue on the edges and seams.

Then he shuffled to the stove and lit the flames under the water and under the saucepan. He just needed to heat the pasta up; it was left over from a day ago . . . so was the gravy. This would take only a few brief minutes to prepare.

Not as it was years ago when the gravy simmered for hours and hours.

Now it is store bought.

He set the plates out on the table, carefully folded a dinner napkin and gently placed it next to the dinner plate on one side of the table, then he set out the silverware and the wine glass. After preparing the first table setting, he set another on the opposite end of the table.

The table was small.

With a careful shuffle of his feet, while the clock struck the top of the hour, he opened the refrigerator and lifted the red wine from the door ledge. He had uncorked it earlier and then chilled it. The corkscrew gave him troubles these days, and he did not want to delay the dinner.

The pasta boiled and the steam rising from both of the saucepans signaled to the old man that it was time. While carrying one dinner plate from the table, he shut the flames off, grabbed the colander and set it inside the sink. With a careful motion, he plopped the pasta into the strainer as the steam rose all around in the kitchen. It fogged the inside of the windows.

It was early November, and the kitchen was cold. Fixed incomes meant that you always wore a sweater.

First, he loaded one plate with pasta and then shuffled to the saucepan and dished out the gravy on the pasta. Then, after setting the plate on one end of the table, he repeated the task for the other dinner plate. Now for the grand finale. Just the same as they did together every Saturday evening for such a long, long time. Why change it now?

The old man shut off the lights and only the candle remained. Romance and candlelight and pasta and wine. The glow captivated his old eyes and warmed his heart.

And the clock ticked, and it danced in time within the quiet stillness.

'Steady now,' were his thoughts while he carefully tugged loose the cork on the wine bottle and with careful movement of his arms, he tilted the bottle over and carefully filled one wine glass, then after steadying his feet, he shuffled over and filled the other glass. He set the wine bottle in the center of the table, pulled out the chair and with a loud groan, the old man finally collapsed into the chair.

"Now, my dear, please, a toast to us," the old man said as he lifted his wine glass in the direction of and in the worship of the empty seat on the opposite side of the table. The old man tilted the glass over and took a long sip.

He set the wine glass down and a single tear rolled out of his eye and landed on the table.

When the tear fell, it landed with an audible sound that mixed in with the rest of the echoes in the quiet stillness.

Spark - Plus Three

Fillin' Up the Freezer

The freezer was large and the two deliverymen had a difficult time carrying it inside and setting it upon the floor of the garage.

"Here is five bucks each for ya trouble. Split it. Thanks!" The homeowner said as he handed them a ten-dollar bill.

"Hey thanks, good luck fillin' it up. Gonna cost a pile of dough to fill that sucker up."

As the homeowner waved goodbye to the men, he whispered, "Nah. It is gonna be full in one shot."

He turned and opened the garage door and entered the house while shouting out, "Honey, the freezer is here!"

He smirked.

"It sure is big," he added while reaching deep into his jacket pocket and fingering the cold hard steel of the grip of the handgun.

"Oh good! I have been waiting for it to arrive," was the answer as his wife reached into the drawer and fingered the cold, hard steel of the grip of the handgun.

"I am so happy it is big. It is going to come in so handy now."

Flash Nine

Hit the Restart Button

"Well, then, since it appears as if none of this makes much sense to me, I guess it is best that I leave now. Before you come gunning for my old ass."

"Just so you know," he said while lifting an eye, and at the same time that he lifted his toastie to take a bite while studying his companion opposite the table from him, "I quit. They did not can my old ass."

"That is not what we heard," his companion said.

"Well, whatever. I quit. Knew those bastards would spread some false rumors. It is all good. I am moving on with a restart in my life. I mean, what the hell was with that picnic and the canoe trip, and the croquet game and that other happy bullshit?"

His companion lifted his beer mug and took a long sip, and when he set it back down on the coaster on the bar counter and smacked his lips, he answered, "Teambuilding. That is what modern, just-out-of-university-sales management does these days. Build a team and get every salesperson revved up and on one page. It works. Or seems to work."

"Works for what? Checking out that pretty girl

from the third floor's ass?"

"Yes, it works for that, but ya know, well, you were doing this for a very long time." Another sip. Another reset on the beer coaster.

"Times change and you didn't."

He picked up his beer and took a sip while pondering his companion's words and statement. He took a bite of the sandwich and set it back down on the plate while saying, "Damn good toastie. Do you like them on brown wheat bread or white? I prefer white but gotta watch my starch intake these days."

"White bread. Only. I always get white. I am younger than you are. I have no issues with eating or watching my diet. I pretty much eat whatever the hell that I want to eat."

He nodded his head, picked up the sandwich and then, before taking a bite, placed it back on the plate.

With another lift of his eye to his companion he asked, "So are you gonna stay on there? I mean with all those silly ding-dongs in charge now and all the changes. Say, ah . . . do you want me to order you a toastie? On white? My treat."

With a mouthful of beer, the companion answered, "Staying on. Jobs are difficult to find these days." With a graceful wave of his hand in the air, the companion added, "I am good. Thanks. Ate a late lunch. You say that you are moving on with a restart of sorts. What do you mean? No offense, but you are a little older and jobs are. . .."

"I am hitting the restart button. The day that I left, I sent out a boatload of resumes, but I was the most successful salesperson there for many, many years and I think these clowns might just give me a call to rethink their stupidity."

"You were the most successful salesperson, like, ah, ten years ago," the companion said as he entered reality into the situation.

Reality hurts.

The companion was honest but he actually was not a friend.

Just then, his cellphone rang. He picked it up, glanced at the number on the screen, and he smiled at the companion.

Flash Ten

Long Legs, Wine, and Beer

It was a hot summer night. You needed to stay hydrated. It was hot, and then it grew even hotter.

When you are a world-famous rock-and-roll superstar, you can have your pick of the women. Young or old, and all of them in between. They flock to you as if you are God's gift to everything. Groupies surround concerts and the after-concert parties like moths to a flame. Except this young woman was not a groupie.

She was anything but a groupie.

To establish a point and in order to clarify the situation and amplify the story, she was only there to do her job. World-famous rock-and-roll-superstars meant nothing to her.

Despite the best efforts of the front man of the rock-and-roll band to attract her attention, she only smiled and went diligently back to her work.

Her use of the English language was not the best; the band member's proficiency of the Hungarian language was even worse, but even with the language barriers, it was painfully obvious that all that this beautiful woman wanted to do was her job and then she would be on her way. There was just a whisper in the broken communication of her being an athlete. You did not need to be a top-notch detective to determine that fact.

Her glorious body confirmed that fact. Her legs were long with a hint of power and muscles. Her hips were slender. Her breasts . . . perfect. Her smile captivating. Her backside . . . perfect.

Then there were her legs. Long legs.

Seemingly endless, in fact. They went on forever and then some more.

Her primary job was to cater the musical event. Before the concert, it was beer, wine, water, and some sandwiches and snacks. Into a cooler and onto a table in the back-of-the-house.

Her inadvertent job was to enthrall the band members and tune up their lust to immeasurable levels. Particularly, the lead front man of the band. His eyes nearly popped out of his head, and it was difficult for him to remain focused upon the looming concert.

A concert that was just a short time away.

Enter stage right. Or left.

When she bent down to load the cooler with the beer bottles, the wine and the water, every man within twenty miles held their breath. Tight shorts, black, silky hair that fell all around her as she worked and that required her to tuck behind her ears, tanned and long legs, a hint of her cotton panties and a whisper of what glory lies underneath the covers.

Her beauty could peel the paint from the walls of the old music house. It sent shivers down the lead front man's spine and made his legs shake.

Yet, all she did was smile at the playful inquires and suggestions embedded within the conversation of the band members and deflect the lust and wave with her delicate, yet powerful hands and dismiss them. The language barrier was easy to hide behind in the process of deflection. Perhaps she understood much more of the language than she pretended to understand.

Perhaps.

It worked for her and did not work for them.

It was obvious that she had a man in her life. A lover. A husband. A lucky man. Very lucky.

The concert went off without a hitch. Perfect. Despite the heat.

The heat of the day and the heat, back stage.

The lead front man thought of her when he sang the love songs. When he performed the ballads. Her vision and impact made a difference. The songs were poignant, honest, and sincere.

Tomorrow, the music critics would rave about the concert performance. Particularly of the performance and abilities of the lead front man for the band. All while not knowing or even remotely imagining the inspiration behind them all.

If only they did. Perhaps, they too, would be rock-and-roll superstars.

Perhaps.

After the concert, in the back of the house, there was no sign of her. Her job was now complete. The sandwiches, snacks and wine and beer were all perfect.

As was she.

The front man went to dinner the next night before they left out of town. To head west. On with the next stop on the tour.

He imagined that every female in the restaurant was she. The greeter, the server, the woman sitting next to him, who laughed too much.

For a second, he thought one of the servers might be her. Did she work a part-time job here? His eyes peered intently in and he studied the woman from afar. Simply a trick of his imagination. It was dreaming on his part.

Sadly, she was not there. Forever, she might haunt him. That was okay; because he would use her as a muse to write songs and elevate his stardom.

Honestly, he would rather have her.

In his arms. In his heart.

Forever.

It was a hot summer night. You needed to stay hydrated. It was hot, and then it grew a bit colder. A cool and welcoming breeze settled in when they arrived at the hotel.

A gentle breeze with a whisper of autumn upon its waves.

The desk clerk had a pleasant smile, but she could not hold a candle to her.

No other woman could ever do so.

Forever.

Flash Eleven

Magic

"You simply need to believe in yourself and you can do magic. Believe me, you will do magic."

Her beloved father sat on the edge of the bed in her cramped little bedroom and he mumbled those words to her.

Her little bedroom might have been the size of Australia right now, or, perhaps it was actually the size of a closet, or it could barely hold her bed, a dresser, and a small chair. It did not actually matter much. If at all.

His smile filled her soul. He made her feel important; he made her feel as if she was the only daughter of a father in the entire world.

His love filled her soul.

Moreover, she believed him. The little girl was only six years old, but to her, her father was a blessing from Heaven and he meant the world to her. Cramped bedroom and illusions aside. Above all, withstanding all, she believed him.

He had no great education, but he had a brilliant mind. What he lacked in formality of education, he more than made up for it in sheer brilliance and in God-given street smarts.

Often in life, that is all that you need.

Her father worked hard, did all that he could do

to provide, to teach, to encourage, to support, to enhance, and to love her and her brother and his wife and his family. He did the best that he could do.

Under the circumstances.

A big old mean city was the setting. Big, old, mean cities can be unforgiving and relentless.

In business, after years of backbreaking work, he lost all that he built. In addition, he lost just a little more.

In life, he never lost his brilliance, nor his street smarts, nor his support, or his unwavering love that filled her soul.

Now he was old. He felt poorly. His body failed him.

Dark times closed in.

Hard times came to the little girl who had grown into a beautiful and amazing and stunning woman with a family, a lovely daughter, a husband, and commitments of her own. There were many bumps along the way, love lost, love gained, yet, love always renewed in so many avenues to her, her eyes opened, her eyes closed, yet her beauty shone through it all.

Her superpower was love.

One day, she struggled to find herself in and amongst the rubble of life. It was desperation.

Dark times.

She needed something. She searched for the answer.

Her father's brilliance shone through the madness, and he reminded her of the magic.

Her magic.

His love, his spirit, his support, his commitment.

The magic.

His words echoed through her soul.

She could do magic, and she did do magic.

She believed, he loved, and that was all that the two of them needed.

He was a blessing from Heaven and in praise and gratefulness; she fell to her knees, opened her arms and her mind, and she thanked God for him, for his love and support, and most of all . . . for the magic.

Her superpower was love, but she also had the magic.

She always did.

Her father was correct.

Spark Four

Faith and Miracles

Humankind created religion and all the confusion that goes with it. God sends us faith and miracles to sort out all the mess that humankind makes.

Flash Twelve

Approach to the Subject

He took two steps to the right and then one half-step to the left. Her eyes in the lens of camera were dark and captivating. The magnificence of her body gave him chills. As he squeezed the shutter, the photographer tried his best to remain focused.

It was extremely difficult.

Her beauty surrounded him and penetrated the lens of the camera. The flow of her body from head-to-toe was not only in his mind, a perfect work of art; it was what he imagined that God envisioned when he created a woman as a companion for man.

The photographer could hear in his mind the voice of his instructor in his advanced photography class, 'Now, always keep in mind the approach to the subject. Portraits can be tricky, particularly if the subject is beautiful as our model is today and diverts your focus. In your mind's eyes, dissect the shot into a graph as I showed you on the instructional video. Use the theory of the parts of the graph for your subject and the background and the foreground. Please do not, allow the subject's beauty or their body parts deflect you from the perfect shot.'

He took the shot. Her beauty surrounded him. Despite his longing and his lust, she was unreachable. After all, he was only a photographer who was capturing images at a moment in time. A moment that has never been before and never will be again. That should count for something.

Actually, it does not count for much, if anything. It was merely a fleeting second in and within the maze known as our world. He captured it with his skill, she enhanced it with her beauty, and he longed for more. He felt as if it would never be.

"What do you see there in your lens of that there fancy camera, young feller?" The old man asked as his dog lifted his leg and peed on a small shrub. A shrub laced with gorgeous early spring blooms.

First off, he was hardly young anymore, and in the back of his mind, he thought how she was so young and he was so old. Despite his best attempts, she was always in his mind and in every shot. The photographer kept telling himself that age was just a measuring stick. That the true age of a person is what is in their heart and soul, not in their birth years. Wishful thinking. She will always look upon him as an old man.

Regardless, she never left his thoughts. How could she?

Secondly, he just took a photograph of that beautiful bloom that the dog just urinated on right before his eyes. Somehow, the photographer felt that was an insult upon an injury.

The photographer pulled out the earbuds that he was using to listen to music in order to get the vibe he needed and to divert his mind from her.

The old man waited for an answer. It seemed as if the dog waited too. The dog sat down next to the old man's leg and looked up at the photographer.

"I am taking autumn shots of these stands of trees. I am trying to work the sunlight through the leaves. It is difficult to find the exact spot. It is all about the approach to the subject.

The old man peered off into the distance and studied the trees. He shook his head.

"I usually just aim and point, and sometimes, I take a damn nice picture."

"That works too."

"Ya sure do have some nice stuff there. Ya look like a pro. I want to hire a photographer to take pictures of Joey and my daughter and me."

The dog stood up when he heard his name.

"Ya do portraits?"

The photographer hesitated and paused, and the visions of her flashed through his mind. It was too much to do right now, for him to move from her glory to taking pictures of this old man, his daughter and Joey. Nothing against them.

"No, sir, sorry. I am just a landscape and a still and object photographer. Generally, I sell them for stock photography."

"Oh well, thanks. Ya seem like a nice feller." The old man shrugged his shoulders and tugged at the leash. "C'mon Joey. Hey, have fun and hope ya get a lot of good ones."

"Thank you. Be safe."

The sunlight fought him the entire way through a progression of fifty shots. It was time to move on down the walking path. Find another copse of trees. With a change of the lens and a different filter and a new set of trees, things began to flow for the photographer. Two steps to the right, three to the left, and he danced with the trees and with the sunlight and the approach to the subject.

The subject did not dance back.

Her soft voice floated through the music in his ears. Despite the softness of her voice, her words might have floated high into the air, through the leaves of the trees, into the wind and off to the blue sky. Into Heaven.

"Wow. Such precision positioning. It looks as if you are dancing with the trees and the leaves."

The photographer removed the earbuds from his ears and turned and faced the voice. Her beauty surrounded him. He smiled, and she smiled in return.

"It is all about the approach to the subject. I am working the sunlight through the leaves."

"I usually just aim and point, and sometimes, I take a damn nice picture."

"That works too."

"You are obviously a professional. Do you do portraits? I am looking for a photographer to do some portrait shots. Are you interested?"

He answered without hesitation.

"Yes, of course." He fumbled with the snaps on his photographer's vest until he found a business card. "Here. Please, let's make an appointment."

She studied the card and nodded and smiled. He smiled back.

He heard their footsteps. He looked up, and she did too. The old man smiled and Joey sat down next to the old man's leg.

Some guilt filtered through the photographer.

"Oh, please, sir, here is my card. On second thought, I will do your portraits," the photographer said as he walked closer and handed them a business card.

"Oh good. I like ya. Hi, honey. I see that ya met my daughter, there young feller. She sure is a stunner. Got the looks from her mom. Not me."

The photographer turned and looked at the young woman. She smiled, and he smiled back.

Flash Thirteen

Picture on the Wall

She still kept his picture on the wall. As to the reason why, she was not too sure of, yet; she did. Most of his clothes remained in the dresser drawers and in the closets, and his belongings remained too.

"The damage is done now. We can't go back to where we were. Ever." Her words cut like a knife. Still, he knew her words were true.

"I know. I understand. Still, if I said the word sorry a thousand times over . . . it still would not reflect how horrible I feel. It was circumstances. No excuses." He spoke the words with his head down, and then he lifted his eyes and then slowly lifted his head to gaze in her direction.

The tears flowed from her eyes and she nodded her head.

"I do understand. I really do. I am to blame too. I am unforgiving at this point. Perhaps, time will change that and perhaps it will not. I do not know. Nevertheless, it changes nothing. We are still back to where we began in this conversation and situation."

There was nothing left to say. No more dead horses to beat. Nowhere left to turn. No ashes or bridges left to burn. Pick the cliché because it did not much matter now. The cliché barrel was now empty.

He turned heels and left. His left hand lingered on the doorknob, there was a pause and he disappeared while gently closing the door behind him as he left.

She thought, 'That was unusual . . . generally, he was right-handed.'

His footsteps echoed on the floor, then on the stairs, and then she heard the sound of the closing of the front door. It seemed as if she had heard that front door shut a million times before this time. Yet, it resounded through a fog of misery and she heard it clearly.

She leaned back on the bed and rested her head on the pillow. It seemed as if all the air in the room left. In fact, perhaps, there was no air left in the entire house.

The last thought she had before sleep overcame her, was that most of his clothes and belongings remained in the dresser drawers and in the closets and his belongings remained too.

That was something she would deal with in the future. Right now, the damage was too powerful, too deep and too fresh. For right now, sleep would bring healing. Or so she thought.

The phone rattled an ominous ring. It woke her from a sound sleep. It was ten minutes to eleven at night. He left about three hours earlier. Almost to the minute.

She tossed the red rose on his grave and wiped a stream of tears away from her eye.

Still, the damage never left.

The authorities could not say if the car ran into

the ditch because of the heavy rain or not. It was supposition at this point.

It was a large oak tree. Immovable. Unforgiving.

The tree seemed as if it was somewhat of an allegory for her tortured soul.

She still kept his picture on the wall. As to the reason why, she was not too sure of, yet, she did. Most of his clothes remained in the dresser drawers and in the closets, and his belongings remained too.

Damage.

A picture on the wall.

It remains.

Flash Fourteen

Tattoo

The little brass bell on the

front door of the store rang. He took his feet off the desk and jumped into action. A customer. She had a paper with a hand drawing scrawled upon it in her hand, and, in her mind, she had a vision.

Damn. She was stunning. He held onto his heart, but it was fruitless. The woman of his dreams stood in front of him.

"There is a little paperwork here and a check on identification required."

She nodded and reached into her purse.

By the rules.

He carefully fixed and adjusted the needle inside the stainless-steel holder and took a deep breath. Perhaps a quick double-check of the settings was in order.

It was.

He placed his hand gently on her spine and began to work. His eyes glanced at the picture, to gather his direction, then to her skin, then to her body and her structure and her beauty. The human body was amazing. Naked skin was just naked skin. Beauty was more than just skin. It was a glorious creation.

He knew that she was gorgeous but, damn, this was overwhelming.

While he worked, he recalled when she walked into the parlor. His breath hitched for a second. When her clothes dropped to the floor, she neatly folded them, and set them aside. He tried his best to avert his eyes.

He failed.

It was just skin. He dealt in skin. Every day. Everyone looked the same.

No, they did not.

Something about love and romance. Inevitable. Inescapable.

Steady now; keep straight as an arrow. No mistakes.

This rose needed to be red and in bloom and perfect.

A touch of water flowing through it. Just a touch.

He needed just a little time. Time escapes us so quickly.

He could not allow her beauty to distract him. Yet, it almost did.

His thoughts wandered as to how the powers to be desperately wanted him to move off the pier. Maybe take a storefront downtown. Close to the seedier side of town. They kept the pressure up. Something about renewing his business license. Holding it up for proper renewals. The man loomed. He would hold his ground.

She jumped and winced. He apologized. Just a hint of her glorious breasts. Concentration, right now, remained paramount.

In his career, he had seen a million of 'em.

'Not like these. . ..'

The rose was red, it was in bloom, and it was not just in one color. He added some hints of green in the leaves and a touch of brown on the stems. More than a touch of blue on the flowing water.

"Done," he said and added, with a hint of caring in his voice, "I am so sorry, about a few deep pinches there. I know it can be a little painful at times. Here let me get a mirror so that you can see it. Here is a towel . . . if you need to cover up in front."

The caring was genuine.

She disregarded his words and popped right up with a smile as he held the mirrors up and she adjusted her body to check out the proper view. Mirror to mirror.

His breath hitched.

Her smile was a mile wide or perhaps a little more.

"I love it! You are so talented and amazing! Thank you. I hope he likes it!"

'He is damn near crazy not to love it. Or to love you too.'

She dressed, thanked him and paid him, and he waved goodbye to her.

He did not stand a chance. Of course, she already had a man in her life.

'Lucky guy. I hope he knows how lucky he is.'

"I cannot believe he was so angry because I inked up. I told him that my goal was to ink my entire body. He doesn't understand me. It is all about him. He is so self-centered."

Her best friend nodded her head in understanding. "These men all are idiots," she added.

The ink was still fresh, her skin was a little sore and the area around the art was still red and while she ran her hand over the artwork and studied it, her mind wandered and her eyes rolled a little from the art to the ceiling, then to her best friend.

"Maybe not all men. The tattoo artist . . . he was dreamy. So hot. All inked up. He was so gentle, so careful. So magnificent. I think that he is the owner of the shop. Honestly, I can't stop thinking about him."

The little brass bell on the front door of the store rang. He took his feet off the desk and jumped into action. A customer. She had a drawing in her hand and a vision.

Damn. She was stunning. He held onto his heart, but it was fruitless. The woman of his dreams stood in front of him.

She checked for any other customers in the shop. There was none. They were alone.

She smiled and unbuttoned her shirt and dropped it on the floor. No folding this time.

He smiled too. He unbuttoned his shirt and dropped it to the floor. No folding required.

The rose was red, it was in bloom, and it was not just in one color. He added some hints of green in the leaves and a touch of brown on the stems. More than a touch of blue on the flowing water.

The ink was still fresh, his skin was a little sore and the area around the art was still red.

They matched perfectly.
Of course, they did.
In so many ways.

Spark Five

Spelling

Always keep your spelling flexible because it invokes fanciful meanderings.

Sort of a Short One

Two Prongs on the Cord

The electrical cord only had two prongs.

The fact that there were only two prongs on the main power cord for the radio did not bother him in the least.

In fact, he was thrilled to see that was the case.

He thought how that was an indication of just how old the radio actually was, and most likely, having only two prongs on the plug and not having a ground prong was a safety hazard. He vaguely recalled from his days of toying with electronics, radios, and televisions, something about the radio chassis potentially being "hot" in terms of electrical voltages because the old power supplies did not have the isolation between the alternating current electrical input voltages and the cabinet and chassis, as did the newer radios. He did not care. When he spotted it on the shelf in the thrift store and the tag stated that the "radio works perfectly" he had to purchase it. It brought back such amazing memories. His father had a radio exactly like this one. It sat on a table in the living room and his father sat in his easy chair next to the radio and carefully tuned the band to listen to music, sports, and the news.

He had vivid memories of his father sitting there in his chair, listening to the old radio while smoking his pipe, while sipping his glass of evening Scotch (poured neat) and he recalled how his father would close his eyes and he would become lost in the magic of radio.

The F.M. radio band did not exist in this era, there was only the A.M. radio band, but the A.M. band could receive some distant stations on clear winter evenings, and a great part of the fun was to see how many distant stations that you could receive. When you heard a weak and distant signal, you would anxiously wait for the announcer to state the radio station's call letters and location. You could dream about visiting such places one day. When you are a ten-year-old boy growing up in Paterson, New Jersey, then, Chicago, Illinois seems as if it might be on the other side of the world.

The static and crackle and pops were all part of the magic of the capturing of the distant signals.

Of all the memories of the old radio, the ones that stuck in his mind the most were of the old radio loudly playing Christmas music during the holiday season. His father always tuned to a station that played continuous Christmas music from Christmas Eve until midnight on Christmas Day and it was pure magic to hear the glorious tunes emitting from the old radio and filling the room and his family's hearts with Christmas spirit. Now, he had a radio just like his father's radio, it was only a few weeks until Christmas Day and he planned to recapture his past by tuning the band at night hoping to capture a station playing Christmas music and filling his mind and heart with magic.

He carefully plugged the electrical plug on the end of a brittle and stiff electrical cord into the wall socket, leaned back in his chair, reached for the on and off switch and turned the old porcelain knob to the on position. A loud "click" and the soft illumination of the glow of the pilot light for the tuning dial told him that power was now inside the radio. A musty smell of dust burning off the vacuum tubes filled the air, and he stood up and readied his hand to pull the plug out of the wall if the radio exploded into flames. The yellow glow of the tubes inside the cabinet added to the magic, and then slowly, a soft rush of static sounded out of the speaker, he sat down, now confident that the radio was not a fire hazard and when he fiddled with the tuning knob, he heard more than static. First, it was a voice then it was a musical jingle for a commercial. It was an automobile dealership peddling cars and the man's face broke into a wide smile.

The incredible magic of this simple radio had brought the man home once more. To the old house on Wayne Avenue in Paterson, New Jersey. To an old living room with wallpaper with flowers and stems printed upon it. He saw his father's face, he smelled the captivating allure of his pipe tobacco, he heard his mother call that dinner was ready and heard the bedroom door of his sister's room upstairs open and close, and then he heard the footsteps of his kid sister upon the staircase of their home.

He was returning home once more. To his family. To their hearts. To the glory of it all.

His smile grew wider and his eyes flickered in the light of the dial lamp as he thought, 'Who needs three prong cords? Newer is not always better. Especially so with radios.'

Short One

Snow on the Capacity Hat

A story from the *Where We Used to Live* collection of stories

First, he grabbed the glass of Scotch (poured neat) and carefully tilted the glass over while enjoying a deep and long swig. Then after a hard swallow and the aftermath of the ensuing, but somehow, strangely enticing burn of the whiskey and after clearing his throat, he grabbed the imaginary microphone and carefully placed his right foot upon an imaginary on-off foot switch located under his desk.

'No pressure on the switch, not yet,' he thought. When the timing was perfect, he pressed down on the imaginary foot switch in order to key the imaginary audio line and within the layers of this amazing fantasy, he spoke into the imaginary microphone with his still deep and melodious voice. A voice, which rode the magical radio waves throughout the airwaves for close to thirty-five years. A golden voice that graced the airwaves until time and change caught up with it and silenced it for what seemed as if it would be forevermore.

"Dell Markle here, and you, my listeners, are here too. On this magical night known as Christmas Eve! We are here together on WTEE where the hits keep on coming! Now, we interrupt our regular programming in order to bring our annual Christmas gift to you! Beginning now at noon on Christmas Eve we will broadcast, thirty-six hours of the most beautiful Christmas music ever recorded . . . with no commercial interruptions. It is our Christmas gift to you." He grabbed the Scotch glass, took a little swig while tapping his fingers on the table and while counting the time beats for the perfect timing of the upcoming announcement, "Except for brief announcements from our sponsors at the top of each hour."

Dell released the imaginary foot switch, and he leaned back in his chair and laughed while pronouncing aloud to the walls of the apartment the success of his imaginary stint on the airwaves.

"The radio listeners never heard that part of the announcement. They only heard the thirty-six hours of the most beautiful Christmas music ever recorded part of the announcement . . . with no commercial interruptions. The, it is our Christmas gift to you, part of my announcement is the only part the listeners heard. Ha! You still are right on top of your game, Markle. Still on top and your old ass still sounds just as good, just as melodious, just as solid as you ever did. You just need one more chance at the microphone. One more chance."

He stood up and wobbled a little. No, to remain

completely factual within the telling of this story, he wobbled a lot.

A helluva lot.

So much so that he held onto the table in order not to fall down.

"Whoaahhh! Easy now there, Markle. Too much whiskey has made you wobbly, and then some too. Careful now. You are only sixty-two years old and you might be a functional alcoholic, but you are not dead yet."

Dell Markle precariously made his way from the front of his apartment where he had what he called his "listening post" set up by a front window, through the small open area of his dining room and after a seemingly long journey he landed in the kitchen. The apartment was only 700 total square feet, but right now, to Dell Markle, it seemed as if he just traveled to and from the ends of the world. It was late afternoon on Thanksgiving Day and the smell of microwaved delicatessen sliced turkey breast lingered in the air. Slices of turkey flopped upon some toast and covered with hot gravy. Hot gravy—fresh from a jar. Dell poured the contents of the boxed stuffing into a bowl, and although he was pie-eyed, rather carefully, he managed to read the directions for cooking the stuffing. With a touch of divine intervention, and a few flips of his fork, Dell successfully managed to prepare the stuffing.

It was a perfect Thanksgiving feast for a washed-up disc jockey who also was a long-time bachelor.

Sliced deli turkey on toast, smothered in a hot coating of jarred turkey gravy, accompanied by boxed stuffing, topped by a blob of jellied cranberry sauce and sprinkled with black pepper. Dell forgot to heat up the can of green beans that he bought and stuffed in a dark corner of the cupboard. They would rather unceremoniously resurface later in the week. Oh yes, it was all washed down with copious amounts of Dell's favorite light beer. Four-ninety-nine for a six-pack at the seedy store on the nearby street corner. A wonderful bargain!

To say that the heyday of the "Cool DJ" was far in the past was somewhat of an understatement. It seemed as if the only thing left from that part of Dell Markle's world was the license plate stamped with "Cool DJ" and screwed to the front and the back of his 1971 Karmann Ghia. His prize Ghia used to be yellow, but now, it was more of a white shade than it was yellow and it had copious pockets of rust near the lower wheel wells, but it actually ran well enough. Thank goodness, because his job stocking shelves and unloading trucks at the local supermarket did not allow too much extra in the way of coins for major repairs.

Dell mumbled, "Screw the light beer, time to go back to the whiskey," while he unscrewed the cap off the Scotch bottle and poured three fingers into the glass. He already was three sheets to the wind, so becoming four sheets to the wind would not mean too much at this point. While he poured the whiskey, his mind wandered back to the glory days when that 1971 Ghia was brand new and he was the total bomb, tooling around town, going through the gears, smoking big cigars, cool sunglasses on, long hair and a beard, and the latest beautiful chick in his rotating gang of groupies seated next to him. He really was the cool DJ! The coolest! His position as the lead DJ on the flagship clear channel A.M. radio station in the big city made him a celebrity. Millions and millions of radio listeners in the New

York, New Jersey, and Connecticut metropolitan area knew his distinctive golden voice. The booming signal from the 50,000 watts of radio power ran down the coax cable and poured into the non-directional antenna farm to spread the signal even farther. The station's chief engineer would proudly display on the station's walls, QSL reception cards from Canada and the west coast and all-over North America and even the Caribbean islands. Celebrities and music stars would stop by and visit with Dell while he was on the air. Dell would spin the latest records from not only the top forty hits but also his stature and status, gave him the ability to play free-form radio, by selecting and playing his own music playlists. When he could do so, Dell played and selected the deep tracks of recordings, the songs and tracks that usually you only heard when you purchased the long-playing album recordings and played them on your own. He was a mixer of playlists, a master of music and a gifted artist who knew what his listeners wanted and they enjoyed. He was really and truly the Cool DJ!

Now, he was a has-been.

Dell Markle wobbled and made his way to the chair at his listening post, with the whiskey sloshing and lapping along the sides of the glass as he teetered and tottered his way to the chair. After a few errant drips of the precious whiskey hit the floor, because of his excessive wobble, Dell slowed his pace and stepped carefully. He made it, flopped down in the chair and scanned the array of radios on the old desk in front of him. His eyes went from the radios to the scene outside his apartment window. The sun was fading now and the day winding down. Up and down the rows of apartments, windows glowed and behind drawn blinds, televisions flickered. Dell almost reached for the knob on the seven-inch television mounted on the edge of his desk, to flip it on and perhaps catch some Thanksgiving football games, but he changed his mind. Instead, he took a sip of his whiskey and flipped the "on" switch for his old, but carefully preserved, tube radio. The old radio covered every kilocycle of the A.M. band and some of the shortwave frequencies too, and more importantly, the radio represented a part of his heritage. No F.M.! Lord knows that Dell Markle despised F.M. because that technology was a large part of his demise.

The tubes warmed up, the soft glow from the tubes and the warm smell of the dust burning off the tubes all combined to tell Dell all he needed to know. His mind raced while he waited for the tubes to bring the speaker to life, and he thought about his journey. It began a long time ago as a youngster when his father's love of radio and his father's career as a radio operator in the military carried over to their civilian world. Together, they built radios from scratch and from kits, tuned the world as ham radio operators, and when Dell went off to a local college, he took communications courses and assisted in the college's operation's radio station on the campus. When he finally had a fill-in opportunity to sit behind the microphone, Dell took full advantage of it. His amazing golden voice combined with his love of rock-and-roll music, and a star was born. Upon graduation, Dell had multiple job offers from radio land and his first stint at a small radio station in rural New Jersey led to bigger and bigger opportunities until he reached the pinnacle of success at WTEE radio, 940 on the A.M. dial. Not only was Dell a showman and master of the microphone, but he was also respected and popular for his vast knowledge of rock-and-roll music. Even with no notes, he could easily rattle off facts and interesting trivia tidbits about music bands and musicians that many stacks of reference books did not contain. Those facts never left him, and despite the dulling of his mind from his excessive booze intake, Dell knew that he could still rattle off music notes and facts from the top of his head that would astound listeners. In addition, he knew many of the musicians and stars personally. Dell remained at the pinnacle until F.M. radio took over with broadcasting music and talk radio and sports became the preferred programming on the static-filled airwaves of the A.M. band.

F.M. was static-free.

The speaker crackled to life and brought Dell back to reality. He slowly tuned across the A.M. band and carefully listened. The sun was almost set now. The day here in New Jersey was cold and the sky was clear. With all the lights out in his apartment, there was little chance of man-made noises and Dell had a chance of catching some far-off stations in DX-land tonight. Dell stopped the dial on a weak station and carefully listened to the signal.

Perhaps he was listening for a ghost from his past, or perhaps he was listening to inspiration for a return to glory.

Most of the present-day radio stations of the A.M. band broadcasted talk radio programs, some sports, religious programs, and news. A.M. radio stations playing music were difficult to find. Even over on the despicable, F.M. band, Dell knew that the band was full of prerecorded or automated broadcasting, all controlled by computer programs and consisted mostly of canned playlists of music, selected by a person with little to no music knowledge and simply based on what the modern media pronounced as "popular." Nowadays, most on-air station hosts (the DJ was a lost label) taped broadcasts far in advance. Dell realized that these hosts now sat in offices rather than radio stations and some of them even broadcasted from home studios and piped the audio feeds in over the internet. How times and technology had changed and combined to make him a dinosaur. Dell heard that there were still a handful of the old guard of free-form disc jockeys on the air, mostly on satellite radio, but his budget would not allow for such luxuries, and right now, if he was forced to admit it, Dell would rather spend extra money on wasting away his liver with doses of booze. The booze numbed him enough and made his life somewhat bearable.

Therefore, instead of any hints of modern technology, Dell used his ancient array of radios and tuned the bands for a hint of past glory remaining out there.

Somewhere.

This evening, Dell's continued tuning across the band brought the same results, and even the dulling of his mind and his spirit with the Scotch could not bring any inspiration for Dell to find what it was that he was looking for. When his fingers caught a hint of music on the airwaves, it was usually Spanish music and he could not understand what the station hosts were saying. With a strong tilt of the glass, the remaining drops of whiskey flowed down Dell's throat and he felt the last burn of the evening. Leaning back in his chair, he flipped the on-off switch of the old radio to the off position and the loud click of the switch was a preamble to the dying glow of the dial lights for the tuning dial. Sadly, there were no ghosts of the past hidden within the magic of the vacuum tubes. The ghosts were long since gone now. Dell stared long and hard as the glow of the dial lights faded away. Somehow, the lights seemed to signify his life. A bright glow, and now it slowly faded away. With a muffled but heavy sigh, he crossed his arms, and thought about how he knew that he had one more stab at a taste of glory in him somewhere. He just knew that he had more to give. Why not? Why not give it another try, and maybe, just maybe, someone out there shares his vision? It all worked years and years ago, and sure, it is a new day and age, filled with the internet, podcasts, gizmos, and gadgets, but why could it not work again? Dell bet that somewhere out there, were still a few old geezers like him that remembered his name, recalled his golden voice and believed that a throwback into a retro era of the golden age of top forty hits and some free-form spins of deep tracks on the A.M. band is worth revisiting. Old geezers spending their lonely Thanksgiving evening, tuning across the radio band, searching for past glory or at least, searching for a purpose in life.

Dell slowly stood up and within his numbness—he felt encouragement. He felt a tingle of a purpose and he felt a hope of a chance at renewal. With renewed purpose, Dell made his way to the storage closet, and he rifled through mountains of boxes, until he found his old cassette tape recorder. He was quite sure that very few people still used cassette tapes any longer, but he did not own any smartphones or audio players to record any voice recordings, therefore, he had to go old school. He had no choice. After all, old school was what this mission was going to be about, and that was perfectly fine for him. Retro. Throwback. Nostalgia. Just about any other word that you could come up with to label his idea for what it was.

Dell laughed as he whispered aloud to his own mind and the walls of the apartment, "Ancient."

Yes, indeed. He would make a demo tape. That was his plan, and, on Saturday, he would head for the library, use the computer there, and with some help from the cute librarian's assistant that he always chatted with, he would write a resume, a cover letter and he would find a list of A.M. radio stations in New Jersey. His demo tape, his resume and his letter would hit the mail, and instead of wasting money on booze, he would spend money on postage and envelopes and cassette tapes. . ..

Technically, tomorrow would be the start of the magical holiday season and Dell hoped for a taste of magic. He lifted the tape recorder out of the dusty box and blew the coating of dust off the recorder. The dust scattered in the air and floated to the floor as if it were clouds of disintegrating reminders of the spent memories and the dust of the past.

Mr. Lloyd Harbaugh poked around the office at the old brick building housing the transmitter power supplies, controls and the studio and operating post for radio station, WLJH. He glanced at the meters on the walls of the control room and shook his head a little. It was a wintry day in northwestern New Jersey; it was early in December and about three weeks before Christmas, and ice and snow can do funny things to the standing wave ratios on the antenna tower. He frowned at the meters because he knew that he would need to make some adjustments because the power output was down.

"Must be snow on the capacity hat," Lloyd mumbled. "Only putting out 400 watts."

Lloyd not only owned the station, he was the general manager, the chief engineer and the only (occasional) on-the-air host who actually would grab the microphone and take a few hours of a tour behind the microphone. These days, Lloyd subscribed to everything else, and the computer controls and the internet automated most of the station's on-the-air-programming. Lloyd's twenty-five-year-old son took care of those duties. That was not Lloyd's bag, nor was it his field of expertise. For the large majority of the station's programming, various organizations and the purchasers of the airtime, taped, produced and created programming off-site and Lloyd's son loaded the programs into the station's automation for the daily broadcasts. His programs and customers were mostly religious organizations with fire and brimstone preachers spouting off religious sermons and warnings in between begging for money, mixed with one guy who was a financial guru handing out investment advice, some nationally syndicated feeds of sports talk, and local feeds for local high school and college sports.

It paid the bills, but just barely. There were no news reports, no weather reports, no live traffic, no morning show hosts, and no evening show hosts. Lloyd had long since stopped producing live broadcasts except for his occasional stints of ad-libs when there popped up holes in the schedules and he could not sell a window of radio time. Then, rather than go silent, he would drag out some old dusty records and spin a few on the turntables like a disc jockey of old. Lloyd only jumped in the operator's seat, when he was desperate, because, as much as he loved old time music and rock-and-roll, his talents on-the-air were limited and shaky at best and his voice not well suited for the microphone. At least Christmas was coming and he could always fill in any holes in the schedules with continuous runs of Christmas music. He paid the royalty fees up front anyway, so the Christmas music often saved the day. Old and steady sponsor's wallets and their monies spent with the station were lean and new sponsors were very rare, listeners were just as rare and the heyday of radio station, WLJH, was now in the past.

As in the very distant past.

He only had to last three more years and he could sell the license and use the money for retirement. Lloyd's son had a full-time job and his interest in the radio station was marginal at best, so the call letters and the legacy would die with the sale of the radio station. That was a reality. A painful reality because the station whose call letters were his own and his father's call letters before him was a labor of true love. At one time, when A.M. radio was king of the airwaves and podcasts and the internet and the streaming of programs were just fantasy pipedreams, there was live programming, there was a full-time weather person, and there were many on-the-air hosts. The station hustled and bustled, and it was a wonderful era. Now, it was a dusty old memory, and he competed with no other stations for ratings and tweaks of money from sponsors because of a boost in the ratings. Years ago, all the station owners and general managers all hung their wallets and incomes on the publication of weekly listener's ratings. Now, he would not even know where to find them, and Lloyd doubted that they even bothered to compile statistics on radio station WLJH. In reality, there were little to none in the way of local A.M. radio stations left with which to compete with any longer.

Lloyd swung the door open to the transmitter room, and he strolled into the room while his eyes glanced at the multitude of meters, pilot lamps, and indicators monitoring the current status of the transmitter and the antenna. A lifetime of monitoring radio frequency energy provided Lloyd with expert skills to determine the status of the antenna and the transmitter by simply gazing at the monitoring devices. With a few glances at the meter readings, Lloyd knew what the trouble was without even entering the deadly transmitter section, where lethal high voltages and harmful RF energies existed. Lloyd only stuck his hands and test equipment in there when it was absolutely necessary to do so. Especially now, at his age, where his hands were not quite as steady as they once were. No, today, it was just the snow on the capacity hat on the antenna tower. A careful tweak of the antenna trimmer and tuners would level out the SWR and allow the power output to reach the maximum peak that his license allowed. He needed to squeeze all the wattage out that he could. After all, 500 watts per daytime and 126 watts at nighttime did not go too far, anyway! His old Gates Model BC1P transmitter had a soft power output tube in the final RF stage, but if it had to, and it was within his license limits to do so, he could pump out a kilowatt of power output. Right now, even with the soft final output tube, 500 watts of transmitter output was easy to achieve with the correct adjustments. That was good because final tubes for transmitters were big bucks. Lloyd slipped his eyeglasses on and he studied the antenna trimmer knobs and with a quick diddle, patience, and some fine-tuning adjustments, the wattmeter worked closer and closer to 500 watts output and Lloyd was satisfied. He knew that when the day warmed up and the sun melted some of the snow on the capacity hat that he might need to adjust the dials again, but for now, he was satisfied. After all, for close to forty years he had fiddled with these stupid knobs on the antenna trimmer, so he could fiddle for a few more.

Currently, the station was broadcasting a religious program with the loudmouthed (in Lloyd's honest opinion) Pastor Derrick Deacon (not his actual name because Lloyd saw the signature on the checks. Somehow, Joe Dale did not work for selling the Gospel over the airwaves) hollering and yelling about repentance because we were in the end times now. His incessant preaching style of fire and brimstone wore on Lloyd's nerves. Lloyd usually kept the audio monitors turned down when the program known as "The Gospel Show of Power and Truth" was on the air. He always ended the program with pleas for more money, and Lloyd knew for a fact that Pastor Derrick Deacon already had a mansion, fancy sports cars and a huge boat docked out of a fancy beach along the Delaware coast. Lloyd wished that he had taken up the Gospel peddling, too.

Satisfied that all was working well with the antenna and the transmitter, and after logging the adjustments and time in the operations logbook, Lloyd wandered into the office and sat down behind his desk. He picked up the daily mail and thumbed through it. Most of the mail were bills that he would struggle to pay and some junk mail, but one large envelope caught his eye. It had handwritten addresses on it and when Lloyd slipped his eyeglasses on over his eyes and Lloyd studied the envelope, he made a note of the fact that the return address was from a small town a few miles north of the station's location, the last name was interesting, and for some reason, it was vaguely familiar.

"Markle. I know that name from somewhere."

Lloyd felt the envelope with his hands because it had an obvious bulge in the center of it, and his curiosity as to the contents had the better part of him. He grabbed the letter opener from his desk drawer, slipped it under the flap of the envelope, and pulled the contents of the envelope out. To his surprise, an old-fashioned cassette tape tumbled into his hands and two typed letters on plain white paper remained in the envelope. He pulled the letters out and his eyes carefully and rather intensely focused upon them. No, okay . . . wait. One paper was a letter and the other paper was a resume. He first glanced at the resume and in bold letters, the name on the top of the resume caught his eyes, and it was then that he knew why the name on the return address was so familiar. After all, Lloyd Harbaugh was the owner of an A.M. radio station, and he was a fan of radio, and he lived and worked in the area all of his life. Now he knew why the name was so familiar. Of course, he knew whom Dell Markle was! Until now, Lloyd never even realized that Mr. Markle was no longer on the air. In fact, perhaps, it was forever since his magical and legendary voice graced the local airwaves. Lloyd had lost track of the legend and he supposed that time and change had swallowed up Dell Markle as it did to so many other wonderful things of the past.

The resume was brief. The heading had his name and his address and his telephone number typed in bold letters along the top of the paper. There was no cellphone number and there was no email address. It was old school, and that was fine with Mr. Lloyd Harbaugh. He did not have any of those, too. The resume carefully and neatly listed a chronological listing of radio stations where the radio legend known as Mr. Dell Markle manned the microphone over his long career.

Lloyd practically laughed aloud when he read the final entry:

'Simply put, I, Dell Markle, am the best damn free-form and top forty spinning, disc jockey who ever graced the airwaves.'

Yes, the resume confirmed that it had been a very long time since Dell Markle had a radio station job. That in itself was a crime, because Lloyd had to agree with Mr. Markle's self-assessment. Dell Markle was the best of the best, and no one sounded as he did behind a microphone or commanded a rock-and-roll music program as he did.

Lloyd anxiously placed the resume aside, and he picked up the other paper, which he now knew was a cover letter to the accompanying resume. Lloyd's eyes narrowed as he focused on the words typed upon the letter.

Although he remained alone in the office, Lloyd felt the need to read the letter aloud. He was not sure exactly why that was, but he did so, anyway. Perhaps it was because these were the words of a radio legend, with the name of Markle, or perhaps, it was a little touch of Christmas magic that tumbled out of the envelope along with the cassette tape.

"To the General Manager of this radio station,

Please forgive me for the impersonal address here, but I have sent out about one hundred of these same exact letters and because of no replies to date, I have long since given up on the notion of a personal response, hence my impersonal address. Nowadays, it seems as the conducting of business has changed to an impersonal world of emails, texts, and hiding behind keyboards. They tell me that this is progress, but forgive me if I label it bullshit. As the great Mr. Joel once wrote and sang, 'And, so, it goes.'

Anyway, the letter that you hold in your hand is one of the last letters that I sent out and in many ways; it represents my last effort and my last hurrah. I realize that many radio stations might not even have general managers any longer, and even fewer have persons that might recognize my name and who I was, and in many ways, I still am. To most, if not all, of the persons, that I wrote letters to, this is a joke and farce, but what I am proposing is a return to the past. To the golden age of A.M. radio, where we ruled the airwaves, where we played the top forty hits and some deep tracks, a time where the sponsors clamored over each other to throw money at us for an announcement of their services, goods and products on the air. I can still do it and in tuning around the airwaves and hearing the wretched condition of terrestrial radio, my firm belief is that a dip into the past will be just as successful, just as lucrative and just as magical as it was back then.

All that I ask for is a chance to man the microphone once more, a chance to sit in the radio shack's chair, a chance to key the transmitter and one, last, chance, to spin a magical assortment of records on a turntable. I still know every aspect of classic rock-and-roll music, and I can spew the notes, facts, and trivia from my mind without any cheat sheets or crib notes. Please, let me pick the music. I can produce the shows all on my own and I will do so without any hourly or salaried compensation. Initially, I only request a commission of the sponsor's monies. If I do a great job and the sponsor's reactions, station inquiries, and listener's responses reflect success, then perhaps we can discuss a wage. I will humbly accept whatever money you as the radio station general manager, feel that might be fair for compensation. You really have nothing to lose, because if I do not muster up any new sponsors, then there is no payout! I realize that giant media corporations now own most radio stations and corporate executives dictate the standard and the rules for airplay. The small independent radio stations, if they exist any longer, might be holding onto a Gossamer Thread, but nothing ventured, then nothing gained.

I believe in this dream, in this plan, I believe in my abilities; I have a great idea for a Christmas Eve to Christmas Day show, which I did many years ago, and I alone, will operate the station and the controls over the holidays. I am confident that the sponsors will love it and all I ask for is the consideration and one more chance. If you have one, please pop the tape in a cassette tape recorder and listen to my demo tape and listen to my voice, and if you agree with my vision and are willing to take a chance, please give me a call. Together, we can once more rule the airwaves. All I need is a small dose of the love that I have been shown in the past to extend to me in the here and in the now.

Thank you for reading this far (if you have done so and I am not gracing your trash barrel by now) and I wish you all the best this holiday season and in the future.

73,

Mr. Dell Markle."

Mr. Lloyd Harbaugh's heart raced in his chest and he grabbed the cassette tape and with the tape in his hand, he practically sprinted to the door of the studio and threw open the door. He knew where an old cassette tape recorder was in the studio and he had to load this tape and push the play button. He already knew that this was his last hurrah too and what his heart had been searching for to fulfill his soul and to return to his roots and to his past too. Maybe, just maybe, Mr. Dell Markle and Mr. Lloyd Harbaugh were kindred souls in their mutual search for fulfillment. After making sure the transmitter feeds and audio controls did not connect to the input for the signal, Lloyd popped the tape into the player and hit the "PLAY" button. In his haste to listen, he could not risk interrupting Pastor Derrick Deacon's daily assault on cowering believers begging for repentance. Lloyd grabbed the headphones, flipped some switches, and the output of the tape player magically floated into his ears.

"Dell Markle here, and you, my listeners, are here too. We are together in radio land. Together, on this magical night known as Christmas Eve here on, radio, WTEE . . . where the hits keep on coming! Now, we interrupt our regular programming in order to bring our annual Christmas gift to you! Beginning at noon on Christmas Eve we will broadcast, thirty-six hours of the most beautiful Christmas music ever recorded . . . with no commercial interruptions. It is our Christmas gift to you."

After a perfectly timed pause, Mr. Markle's magical voice floated into Lloyd's headphones once more. "Except for brief announcements from our sponsors at the top of each hour."

Lloyd reached out and hit the "STOP" button on the player. He did not have to listen any longer. Dell Markle's magical voice was still just as golden and as perfect as he recalled it when it floated in on what seemed as if it was every A.M. radio throughout the airwaves of three states and some more. He leaned back in the operator's chair at the main post in the studio and envisioned the glory of having Mr. Dell Markle gracing this chair and manning the controls. A radio legend reaching out to the past for one last gasp. Lloyd understood, and he knew that his son would think that he was totally off his rocker. Maybe he was, and maybe Dell Markle was too. Somehow, as crazy as it all seemed, it had a ton of potential and some logic associated with it too. And a touch of Christmas magic, too. Lloyd popped the tape out. He had a sudden thought to hit the audio button for the station monitors to listen to the broadcast signal, and immediately the booming voice of Pastor Derrick Deacon filled the studio.

"Furthermore, if you commit your life to what is good and just and kind, then surely, the Lord will show you the way to the pathway to your heart and give you joy and peace. Do not stop, dear listener, continue to charge ahead until you find your destiny and the Lord will make your life whole and bring you home!"

Lloyd smiled, and he stood up and ambled to the office.

"Maybe this guy is not such a fraud after all," Lloyd mumbled.

He picked up the resume for Dell Markle off his desk and then picked up the handset of the telephone in the office and after looking at the telephone number . . . Lloyd carefully dialed the telephone.

Lloyd Harbaugh parted the shabby curtain on the front window of the office at the brick building labeled with a small, hand painted sign proclaiming this to be the proud headquarters for A.M. radio station, WLJH. Despite the recent cold wave and snowy weather, Lloyd heard the sound of car tires hitting upon the gravel and stone of the driveway in front of the building. Some stone and gravel did not freeze in place yet. He knew that today was the day. Today was going to be the beginning of an experiment, or an adventure, or a new direction, or it might just be a total and complete failure . . . regardless, today was the day.

An old car had pulled up in front of the building and Lloyd did a double take at the appearance of the vehicle. It was an old sports car, a Karmann Ghia, if he recalled his old cars correctly, and Lloyd was pretty sharp regarding identifying old cars. The license plates on the car were clear and pronounced in its proud proclamation. They were custom, New Jersey license plates, the plates defined a New Jersey attitude, and Lloyd surmised that they defined the owner of the vehicle too.

COOL DJ, blinked loudly and clearly to Lloyd and he smiled after reading the license plate's proclamation.

Lloyd walked out of the doorway of the office; he flung open the door and stood on the small front stoop of the building. He waited on the stoop for the driver of the vehicle to park the vehicle and shut off the engine. It was a cold morning and northwestern New Jersey had received a slight dusting of snow overnight, just enough to coat everything with a perfect dusting of winter white. The old car was once a yellow color, but Lloyd noted how time, age, and the weather had now caught up with the vehicle. Now the vehicle was practically white, with some faint hints of yellow and some rusty spots in and around the wheel wells. Regardless of its battle scars, the car was very cool, and somehow, it all fit the image that Mr. Dell Markle should arrive on the scene to begin a nostalgic adventure by driving a nostalgic automobile.

Lloyd stood and waved as Mr. Dell Markle exited the vehicle and he smiled and waved back. Lloyd thought how Dell was much taller and leaner than he envisioned. Mr. Markle had graying and thinning hair, and a neatly trimmed salt and pepper beard and mustache. Dark eyes enhanced his thin and long face. He was a handsome man. Dell carried a small canvas bag with him.

"Good morning, Mr. Markle," Lloyd extended an initial greeting and then added, "You are early. Very early."

Dell Markle laughed a little and waved at the dusting of snow on the ground while saying, "There was this dusting of powder on the ground and there is no way that I would be late for my first radio gig in eighteen years!"

Lloyd thought how his golden voice sounded even

better in person than it did over the airwaves floating out of the finest speakers.

The two men shook hands and Lloyd said, "I understand. Welcome to radio station, WLJH. It is my pleasure to meet you in person. By the way, nice car."

"Believe me, the pleasure is all mine. I am still trying hard to recover from the shock of your phone call and your offer. Thank you, truly, with all of my heart for giving me a chance. Thank you for believing in me. This is a dream that has come true." Dell turned and pointed at the car, and his eyes narrowed and squinted. His thinning hair moved in the gentle breeze of the cold morning and sensing the movement, Dell reached up to smooth it out on top of his head. Dell said, "Ah, the car, yes, it is a veteran of many adventures and journeys. Quite literally. It is very much as I am, a product of a bygone era, but we are returning to glory, and someday, the Ghia will too."

"Come on inside. I know it does not look like very much from the outside, but hopefully, the inside will look more inviting and somewhat familiar."

The two men walked inside the building. Lloyd first showed Dell around the office area, and then he showed him a pictorial history of the station that he kept with a scrapbook of photos, news clippings, and general information on the station. Finally, since they still had some time to kill before airtime, over a cup of coffee, they discussed the history of the station, both where it was then and where it was now. When Lloyd noticed Dell glance at his wristwatch and then watched as his eyes darted in the direction of the door marked "Studio" then Lloyd knew what was on Dell's mind.

"Ah, yes, you want to see the operator's post and prep for your shift. I think you will see that the controls are very basic. I hope that they are very familiar to you. I can stay and help with controls until you become accustomed. As I mentioned, I have an extensive music selection on vinyl and loaded on the computer too."

Dell nodded, turned, and pointed in the direction of the front of the building to indicate where he parked his car. "I have some of my own vinyl collection with me. It is in the car in an old cardboard box. The same box that I used when I packed them up in and left my job . . . eighteen years ago. With all due respect, I am not going to do too well, fiddling with computers to dial up music. Please, let me spin 'em."

"I understand. That is a large part of the plan. Part of the vision. To spin your own. I agree. We can go and get them in a few minutes. You still have an hour and a half until airtime. Let's go in. I have to check the output of the transmitter, anyway. You know, we had the snow and all."

To Lloyd's surprise, Dell responded with a nod of his head and an acknowledgement, "Yes, snow and ice on the capacity hats. I remember these snowy mornings and watching the meters. I have, or I guess that it is a bygone requirement too, so I will say, I *had* a first-class radiotelephone license. I can make adjustments too." Dell downed the rest of his coffee. He set the cup back on the desk when Lloyd waved to leave it there, and Dell stood up and picked up the small canvas bag and waited for Lloyd to lead the way.

Lloyd smiled and mumbled, "Capacity hat. We only have one tower and one hat. Only five-hundred watts daytime and a measly one-hundred and twenty-six watts after sunset. It does not go too far."

"Any takers on sponsors?" Dell asked while he followed Lloyd through the door leading to the studio and the control room.

"Just a bicycle store and repair shop over in Warren. He used to be a regular until a few months ago, and then he disappeared. I gave him freebies for this morning. The copy for the advertisement is on the desk in there. He wanted to listen in, and then he would decide if he would commit. It is going to be a lean and mean few paychecks and bank deposits for both of us." Lloyd put his hand on Dell's shoulder and added, "He said that he was open to sponsoring the show but he was very honest and said that he never heard of you." Dell nodded and Lloyd studied his face for a reaction before adding, "He is very young."

"Yes. Very young. I understand. No hard feelings. After today, the phone will ring off the hook. I can feel it."

"Well, here it is," Lloyd, said as he opened the door to the studio and the two men stepped into the room.

Dell stopped short in his tracks. Lloyd heard a low whistle escape from Dell, and then he heard him take a deep breath and slowly exhale. In studying Dell's face, Lloyd realized that this must be an incredibly emotional experience for Dell. A return to his past. A revisiting, but in many ways, a reawakening. A reunion. Perhaps a renewal.

Dell's lip trembled, and some tears licked into the corners of his eyes, but he maintained his composure. Lloyd could not even imagine the memories that this moment must be inspiring within Dell Markle. When you love what you do to earn a living in this world, then it somehow invades your soul and becomes a part of you that never leaves. Lloyd tried hard to imagine what it was that Dell was feeling right now, while standing in a studio and a radio station's control room for the first time in eighteen years, after spending a lifetime in these types of rooms and at the helm in front of the microphone. And to be put out to pasture and left for dead seemed so unfitting an end for such a talented man. It was something that Lloyd took for granted, being in the studio every day, seven days a week and for all of these years. Lloyd had spent forty-two years working the station, and in his mind, he quickly switched places with Dell and realized that he would have the same reaction. Lloyd remained silent as Dell recovered and he watched while Dell slowly walked over to the main operator post and he ran his fingers gently over the back of the chair parked at the main console. After a few moments of silence while Lloyd allowed Dell the peace to take it all in, Dell spoke first. He pointed to the on-the-air sign, which was illuminated, and the VU meters on the main control console that bounced and hopped in time with the transmission. From a lifetime of studying such meters, Dell knew what that particular hop and bounce meant.

"Spoken voice? No music? What program is on the air now, Lloyd?"

"It is a canned program. A purchaser of airtime. In fact, our most lucrative purchaser of airtime. Pastor Derrick Deacon. A hell fire and brimstone preacher guy. We have no weather person, no news reports, no traffic reports, and obviously very few sponsors. I am betting the farm on you and this idea. It is your last hurrah and it just might be mine too. I think that I would have already sold the license and station if not for Pastor Deacon and some other purchasers of airtime. They keep us afloat. Pastor Deacon is not too happy with our plans for the thirty-six hours of continuous Christmas music. The other stations that he syndicates with, all jumped at his Christmas message and gave him lucrative airtime. I thought for a few moments that he would cancel with us, but he hung in there since our area of coverage is unique for him and he has some dedicated listeners to our station. Dedicated listeners equal donations. Since we are beginning the special program on Christmas Eve, it will push his Christmas message off until after midnight on what is technically, the day after Christmas. He is taping a special Christmas Eve message for before you go on the air at noontime on Christmas Eve. I promised him a discount. My son loads all of his programs for the week into the computer and the computer automates the shows. Right now, we are on autopilot until you take over at the top of the hour. I keep the audio monitors off in the office and control room. The truth is that I find the pastor very annoying."

Now seemingly recovered from the waves of emotions and flashbacks, Dell smiled and nodded his head and then pointed at the console and asked, "I understand and once again, thank you for your faith in me and our visions. May I? I think I already know all of these controls. I will not touch anything. This is all very similar to a number of boards that I ran for many years. Especially the little station where I first started. This microphone is a beauty."

"It is. Great frequency and audio response. I cannot wait to hear your golden voice on it. Please do sit down and relax. I can give you the scoop once you settle in and study it."

Dell pulled the chair out, set his canvas bag on the floor next to the chair. He reached over and unzipped it and pulled out a pair of old headphones. Lloyd smiled when he saw what it was that Dell had in his bag.

"I brought my own cans. I have had them for years. I hope that you do not mind. I don't leave home without them. They fit my head perfectly. They are very well broken in too." Lloyd did not answer with words, only with a nod and a smile. He was in admiration of this man. A radio legend. A true professional. Of course, he would bring his own cans.

Dell wiggled in the chair a little and his eyes were at first, very wide, then they grew dim and tears filled them once more because the emotions returned.

Lloyd walked over, placed his hand on Dell's shoulders, and asked, "You, ok? Does it feel good?"

At first, all that Dell could do was to nod his head because the words would not come.

He wiped at his eyes then spoke in a halting voice, "I am sorry for the loss of emotions and composure. I promise that I will pull it together at airtime. I will not let you down. It feels wonderful. I cannot even express what I am feeling right now after all of these years. My dreams, my hopes, and my prayers fulfilled for one more ride behind the microphone."

"Dell, I need to remind you that the station is only putting out 500 watts daytime and one-hundred and twenty-six at night. An eyedropper of the power that you used to have at your fingertips."

Dell's head turned, and he faced Lloyd while speaking with a low volume but with raw emotions.

"It would not matter if it was five watts QRP. It does not matter to me. Honestly and frankly, I fought my inner demons and became sober for this opportunity. I am reborn. This is home. Where I used to live. There is little doubt that I have come home for Christmas."

The words and emotions of the moment stole all of their words.

Lloyd allowed Dell a few minutes to study the board and the controls and he asked for his car keys, went out to the car, brought the vinyl records into the studio, and set them on the floor next to the turntables. After an extensive review of the controls and the board, (of which Dell already knew and explained some of the controls to Lloyd before Lloyd could even explain them) the two men went off to the transmitter controls and adjusted the antenna trimmer. They had to peak the transmitter's output and knock that annoying snow off the capacity hat. It was ten minutes to nine in the morning. When Dell settled into the chair, he selected a handful of vinyl records and had them poised and ready to spin on the turntables. After some last-minute details, Dell announced that he was ready to go.

"Dell, do you want me to hang here in the studio with you? I can watch over your shoulder and help with the buttons if you need it? Or I can go behind the glass and hang out in the control room?"

After hearing Lloyd's words, and the posing of the questions, Dell's head whipped around and a wide smile formed on his face.

"Behind the glass? As if you are the engineer and the producer and such?"

Lloyd knew that right now, Dell returned to a time long ago, when he had a full staff that supported his show, and his broadcast, and he felt a shiver go down his spine at the sincerity in his question and the meaning behind all of it.

"Yes, Dell. I will be the producer and the engineer and the assistant too."

"Then behind the glass, it is. We can chat back and forth with this button and some hand signals, right?" Dell pointed to a button on the control board.

Almost in a whisper, Lloyd answered, "Yes. That button. You will be on manual. Just like the old days. As you said you are back home where you used to live. You have four turntables, two cassette tape players, and two reel-to-reel players. Even old-time paper copy for reading ad and info and breaks. As I mentioned before, the copy for the bicycle shop ad is there on the desk. Right for now, unfortunately, that is our only sponsor. You might need to ad-lib some time with your incredible music knowledge. Our main phone number, the weather report for today and a schedule of upcoming broadcasts is there in paper copy too. Do you need anything else for now? I can count you in. We have two minutes."

"I am good. Thank you. I am ready to go."

Lloyd extended his hand, the two men shook hands, and Lloyd whispered, "Good luck," and he turned and exited the studio. Dell took a deep breath. He fingered the microphone button, played with the foot switch and decided that until he had a good feel of the foot switch that he would use the console microphone button to key the audio. Taking a deep breath, Dell gently slipped the headphones on over his head, opened the audio feed, and he listened to the last words of hell fire and brimstone from Pastor Derrick Deacon.

It was show time. Finally.

Dell turned and watched the last second click off on the clock, and he turned and watched as Lloyd held his hands in the air and counted down until the last finger shook and waved. Lloyd pointed at Dell that he was good to go.

'This was all surreal,' Dell thought as he slid the microphone switch to open the audio feed and all sense of any nerves immediately left him. It was just as he said before . . . he was home.

Where he used to live.

"Good morning, radio listeners everywhere! Welcome to Morning with Markle on WLJH 670 on the A.M. dial. Dell Markle here, with my wing-man, Mr. Lloyd Harbaugh, behind the glass. We've knocked the snow off the capacity hat, tuned the antenna, warmed a cup of coffee or two, and here we are, all set to keep you company on this cold and snowy morning. Hello, Warren County and Easton, Pennsylvania and Sussex County and wherever it is that you are listening to my voice today." After a slight pause, Dell timed his voice and reentry perfectly, "We are proud to return to the airwaves here at WLJH, eighteen years after my microphone last went silent. Some old radio listeners might remember me and if so, thank you! To all the new listeners, welcome to old time free-form radio with a touch of old-time top forties. If top forties even, exist any longer! If not, we will pick 'em and spin 'em. We are happy to bring you free-form radio at its very best. No canned playlists, no endless commercials, I will return you to the good old days of A.M. radio when the top forty hits ruled the snap, crackle, and static of the airwaves. I pick the music and you can always give Lloyd and Dell, a call at nine-oh-eight-two-six-four, seven-seventy and make some requests for special music, we will give you the inside scoop on the history behind the songs and together, we can take a trip down memory and nostalgia lane! Here at WLJH the listeners are in charge. Now, right before we get into some continuous free-form music radio, here is a quick word from our sponsor."

Dell effortlessly glided into the commercial, and Lloyd marveled at Dell's talent. He rushed to grab his own set of headphones and he plugged them into his control board because Dell's voice was so glorious to hear. It was as if his voice floated on the airwaves and captivated your ears. Lloyd was sure that any listeners out there welcomed the commercial and listened to every word. You could hardly tell that Dell had even moved to the words from the sponsor. He was that good. No, he was great!

"Speedy's Bicycle Shop over in Warren gives you a good deal and a good deal more too! The best in cycling, at the best prices with his famous first-class service and his reputation of always putting the customer first! It is Christmas time and Speedy is manning the sales floor and the shop and waiting for you to come on down to pick out that perfect set of wheels for Christmas. Forget the big-box stores and their impersonal service! Come on down to Speedy's where you are treated like a friend and a valued customer too! Give Speedy a call right now, at nine-oh-eight-two-seven-nine-three-five-oh-nine or better yet, ride on down to thirteen-twelve Main Street in Warren and check out the selection and service. This is old fashioned downtown shopping during Christmas and beyond too! Once you stop by Speedy's you will never shop anywhere else for your cycling needs. Plus, you are supporting our local businesses! Unbeatable! There is free parking is available behind the store in the rear of the shop. Be sure to tell Speedy that Dell Markle over at WLJH sent you. Merry Christmas from Speedy's Bicycle Shop and all of us here at WLJH."

Lloyd leaned back into his chair and his smile was a mile wide. Dell had added to the commercial copy, he had adlibbed a great deal of that commercial, greatly embellishing upon the original copy, and Lloyd knew that it sounded great. He pulled his headphones off, flipped the audio monitors on in the control room, and marveled at the golden voice of Mr. Dell Markle. The VU meters bounced in perfect time as if they were the legs of a precision marching band, making their way down a football field at halftime, the tower pumped out five-hundred glorious watts of non-directional RF energy and Lloyd was as giddy as a drunken man was late on a Friday evening. This was old time radio! In every way, and in every bounce of the meters! This man sitting in the operator's chair in front of the control console sounded as if he never left the airwaves eighteen years ago.

Instead, he sounded as if it was eighteen hours

ago!

"Now, back to the show. Listeners out there, let me tell you that there is no better way to celebrate my return to the airwaves than to play a cut from the golden age of Christmas music and a song that seems so perfect for today's emotions and mood. Here is the Chairman of the Board, one of New Jersey's finest, Frankie S, with his classic vinyl version of 'I'll Be Home for Christmas,' spinning with the authentic needle pops and crackles on the turntable here at WLJH."

Dell masterfully dropped the vinyl on the turntable, directly on the selected cut; he flipped the microphone off and perfectly cut in the number one turntable as the first glorious music notes began to play. Lloyd was amazed! Dell spun in his chair, smiled wide and gave an emphatic two thumbs up signal to Lloyd, who immediately returned the smile and the signal from behind the glass.

And it was then that the phone rang in the main office of radio station, WLJH. . .. It was Ray from Speedy's Bicycle Shop on the telephone, exuberantly asking how he could sponsor the Morning with Markle Show. Lloyd laughed, and he carefully began explaining some details to Ray, when suddenly, another line lit up on the telephone, then another, and then the last line lit up on the telephone too. There had not been four lines lit up at the same time at radio station WLJH in twenty years.

Maybe in thirty years.

Lloyd had four lines going at once, but he only had one pair of ears and hands. . ..

There now remained little doubt that this was going to be a monumental and memorable day!

Lloyd Harbaugh parted the brand-new curtain with the custom embroidered call letters of WLJH and their brand-new logo sewn in them, that was hanging on the front window of the office at the brick building labeled with a small, hand painted sign proclaiming this to be the proud headquarters for A.M. radio station, WLJH. Despite the ongoing cold wave and the string of consecutive days of snowy weather, Lloyd heard the sound of car tires hitting upon the gravel and stone of the driveway of the station. Some stones stubbornly remained unfrozen. Lloyd smiled when he saw it was Dell Markle's now familiar Karmann Ghia pulling in for a soft stop in the reserved parking spot in front of the station. Right next to Lloyd's reserved spot. Lloyd had a helluva time trying to pound the signpost with the sign stenciled with "Cool DJ" on top of it into the cold and frozen ground. Lloyd gave up, and for now, he temporarily stuck the signpost in a plastic bucket of cement and planned to mount it into the ground in the spring when the ground thawed.

He glanced at his wristwatch and mumbled, "Still an hour early too."

The front door opened and Dell walked in, stomped his boots on the walk-off mat, and kicked the snow off the heels.

"Good morning, Dell. How was the ride in?"

"No issues. The wheels are old, but they actually do pretty well in the snow. Finding an apartment closer to the station helped too. It is just this side road here," Dell turned and pointed out the window to indicate the road outside the station leading to the driveway, "the town ignores us. Merry Christmas Eve, Lloyd."

"Yes, merry Christmas Eve. Well, the town might ignore us, but our listeners and our sponsors have not. You should see the emails and the letters coming in. It is remarkable. I even had to fish around in a drawer in the storage closet to find our old QSL cards to answer a card request." Lloyd fished around in the stacks of papers on his desk, found the QSL reception-reporting card and held it up for Dell, who smiled widely at the sight of the card. "It's from a ham radio operator in Alberta Province in Canada who tunes medium wave at night. Picked us up with our measly one-hundred and twenty-six watts. Says we were five and five on his signal meter."

Dell nodded, pursed his lips, and narrowed his eyes. "Not too bad. It pays to tune out that snow on the capacity hats. Ah, ah . . . capacity hat."

"It does, say, Dell, this has been wildly successful beyond our wildest dreams and you have been slamming it for three weeks straight. I just want you to know what all of this means to me, to my son and I and our families . . . you do not have to fly solo on this Christmas Eve show. My son told me that he could record your voiceovers and the top of the hour introductions and the sponsor announcements and such. He is fully capable of putting the entire show on autopilot. He has

Christmas music playlists all set to go now. You can go home, listen, and relax. I mean, especially, at night when we reduce power. Thirty-six hours is a very long gig, even for you and even if there will be minimum talking. You deserve a break, and after all, it is. . .."

While Lloyd spoke and made his suggestions, Dell was fervently shaking his head to indicate a resounding "no" to the ideas. Dell Markle was polite and did not interrupt his boss, but when Lloyd saw Dell's reaction to his words and his suggestion, his voice drifted off on its own.

"No, Lloyd, thank you and thank you to Mark, too. I will not do anything but a live broadcast for the Christmas Eve and Christmas Day show. I promised our listeners and the sponsors too, and I have been publicizing this show for a week now. Some old timers out there in radio land might even recall, the old show, Christmas Magic with Markle, and I plan to duplicate it to the very last detail."

"I understand, Dell, but what about spending Christmas with your friends or your family?"

Lloyd had never heard Dell mention any family, friends, or a wife, or a woman in his life or, in fact, any social life at all, and when he spotted Dell's reaction to the question posed, Lloyd instantly regretted asking it. Dell's face grew pensive and his eyes wandered around the station's office. First, they wandered out to the window to the control room and then to the studio and finally, they landed upon the operating console and the control board. A touch of tears filled the corners of his eyes, and Lloyd watched as Dell wiped them away.

"I have no family and friends other than everyone out there in radio land. My listeners are my brothers, my sisters, my uncles, cousins, my friends, my wives, and my family. I need to give them what they gave me this Christmas and what you gave to me. A gift of joy. A gift of my own heart. This is where I want to be for the holiday . . . with my family. Now, Lloyd, you take the days off and enjoy it with your family . . . Dell Markle is on the air."

Lloyd stood there, studying Dell for a few seconds, and then he nodded his head and made an effort to break the emotions with a touch of business.

"First thing this morning, I fiddled with the antenna trimmers. Added more capacitance. Ya know . . . some snow on the capacity hat. You should be good, with the sun coming up, but the prediction is for heavy snow tonight and tomorrow. Full weather report copy is on the desk in there for you to read on the air for the morning show. This is going to be a real white Christmas, so you will need to diddle the antenna trimmer quite a bit. I stocked up the coffee, tea, water and some soda in the fridge and some frozen dinners for the microwave."

"Thank you. A white Christmas will be perfect. Very nice. I am looking forward to it. I appreciate that, and how about the sponsor's announcements?"

"Oh yes, all the copy is on the desk in there for the entire show. Mark is on top of his game now, and I noticed a real change in him as of late. Suddenly, the station is of huge interest to my son and my daughter-in-law too. They will be in today to help with the phones and emails until you begin the special Christmas show. Mark even hinted at trying to sit with you and learn to take a shift or two behind the microphone. By the way, old man Davidson at the First National Bank has been a glorious, but persistent pain-in-the-ass. He called already today, still trying to barter to buy all the Christmas Day advertising times for the entire noon to six o'clock segment. When I told him that we already booked all the slots and it would not be fair to all the other sponsors, well, he offered to triple the price. I still had to let him down gently."

"Awesome on Mark. Anytime he wants to co-host the show—then let's go for it! Ha! Old man Davidson! Yes, he is an old fan of the show and remembers it rather well. Plus, he has deep pockets too."

Lloyd admired Dell's enthusiasm, but he realized that some business was at hand; therefore, Lloyd deepened his voice and spoke his thoughts without wading too deep into business to spoil the festive mood of this special day.

"Dell, ya know, after Christmas, we need to sit down and seriously renegotiate your salary and commission."

Dell's eyes grew wide, and he walked over to the small coffee station and held up a mug in the air to ask Lloyd if he wanted a cup of coffee. Lloyd nodded, and Dell prepared two cups. As he did so, Dell's enthusiasm grew as his voice grew louder with the details of his Christmas show.

"Yes, we certainly can discuss that. After Christmas. First off, let's see how these days go along before we do so. I have to tell you, Lloyd, this is going to be some show. I have stacks of old vinyl from the golden age of Christmas music, some tapes of more music from my old archives, I will read a little from Dickens' *A Christmas Carol* with strategic excerpts and I always read, *The Night before Christmas* poem around nine at night on Christmas Eve. It is a tradition and the listeners go nuts over that." Dell turned and winked one eye and added, "I use my best voice." He poured the mugs full of piping hot coffee, added sugar and milk, walked the cup over to Lloyd, and handed it off. They held the mugs in the air in an informal toast and Dell continued to explain, "Another highlight is at midnight when Christmas Day blooms, I play the entire Hallelujah Chorus." Dell grew animated and his joy was readily apparent as his voice grew intense and his free hand waved in the air.

"Lloyd, I did not tell you 'bout this one, but get this . . . I went out on the sly, made contact with and had our buddy, Pastor Derrick Deacon, record a reading of Luke's Gospel with the Christmas story to play right before the Hallelujah Chorus begins, ya know, I had to soften his soul over preempting his usual Christmas program! Pastor Deacon is thrilled."

"Nice! You know, Pastor Deacon has been growing on me as of late. I even occasionally leave the audio monitors up on his show these days . . . speaking of which," Lloyd pointed at the clock indicating that it was time for Pastor Deacon's daily program of dire warnings, imminent hellfire reining down upon us all, and his general huff and puff to end and for Morning with Markle to go on the air.

"Oops, I am on it," Dell said while glancing at his watch and while he turned toward the studio door, he added, "oh, yes, I love the curtains too." Dell pointed at the new curtains and disappeared into the studio to begin the show.

Lloyd smiled, walked to the control room, and sat down behind the glass as Dell opened the show. Lloyd leaned back in his chair and sure enough, two minutes into the show, the telephone lines all lit up with calls.

"I hope that Mark and Dana get here soon. It is going to be a crazy busy show. I gotta talk to Mark about a bigger telephone board here and maybe some part-time help to answer it."

It was noontime on Christmas Eve, and Mr. Dell Markle was at the microphone manning the station and the controls of WLJH.

He now used the foot switch to key the audio.

"Happy Christmas Eve to all the listeners, both new and old out there in radio land! This is Dell Markle at the microphone for radio WLJH, six-seventy on the A.M. dial and welcome to the annual Christmas Magic with Markle show! I, Dell Markle, will be your host and the announcer and engineer and producer for this special show, with the best in free-form radio found anywhere on the A.M. dial! For the next thirty-six hours, I will spin some vinyl and flip some tapes from my own personal collection of music from the golden age of Christmas music and the best of radio. This is the perfect backdrop for your Christmas celebration. And, you do not want to miss the special Christmas message and blessing from our own Pastor Derrick Deacon at midnight when Christmas Eve gives way to Christmas Day! First, I would like to thank radio station owner, Mr. Lloyd Harbaugh, his wonderful wife, Becky, his son Mark, and the entire Harbaugh family for the opportunity to be sitting here today. I thank them from the bottom of my heart. Then, I want to thank our loyal sponsors and most of all, all the faithful listeners out there in radio land! You have already made this a magical Christmas and an unforgettable three weeks or thereabouts in my life since I began the Morning with Markle daily show here on WLJH. Now, we move into the Christmas show, where we will broadcast, thirty-six hours of the most beautiful Christmas music ever recorded . . . with no commercial interruptions. It is our Christmas gift to you." He grabbed his coffee mug, took a little swig while tapping his fingers on the table and all the while counting the time beats for the perfect timing of the announcement, "Except for brief announcements from our sponsors at the top of each hour. Our glorious show is brought to you by, Speedy's Bicycle Shop. . .."

At midnight, when Christmas Eve turned into Christmas Day, Dell Markle pushed the correct button for playing a prerecorded message and the booming voice of Pastor Derrick Deacon thumped through the speakers. Dell smiled and stood up and stretched. Twelve hours into the marathon and he was feeling wonderful. He had about forty-five minutes to kill, while Pastor Deacon delivered his Christmas message and the Hallelujah Chorus played. It was time for a cigar to celebrate the arrival of the best Christmas Day ever. Dell walked out of the studio, through the control room, and out to the office. He was alone in the radio station building, but on the other side of the antenna tower, there was a world of friends and family with him. That was part of the magic of radio. You never knew who was listening out there! The small

Christmas tree that Dana and Mark setup in the office happily twinkled at Dell while he slipped his winter coat on and opened the front door to stand on the front stoop of the building and enjoy his cigar. The booming voice of Pastor Derrick Deacon thumped out of the audio monitors in the office, and Dell left the door ajar to keep an ear on the broadcast. Pastor Deacon was in fine form for his Christmas message!

"Chapter Two of the Gospel of Mark, tells us the glorious story of the birth of Jesus Christ, dear friends, and it came to pass in those days, that a decree from. . .."

Dell pulled the cigar out from his coat pocket, took his pocketknife out and sliced the end off of it, pulled out his lighter and lit the smoke with a few hard draws. The exhale of smoke gathered up and around his head, and then it disappeared into the cold Christmas air. It was snowing rather heavily. There was about six inches of snow on the ground already, and the prediction was for about twelve inches of snow to fall before it ended on Christmas afternoon. Christmas travel would be havoc, but this scene was picture-postcard-perfect. Dell took it all in, the snow falling, the coating on the ground and on the shrubs and on the evergreen trees lining the small driveway at the entrance to the station. Dell drew another puff on his cigar and he thought about how he would not want to be anywhere else in the entire world rather than where he was right now. He had come such a long way in such a short amount of time. All because of a dream. A vision, and now he left deli-sliced turkey and lonely apartments in the rearview mirror.

However, Dell did keep the magical old tube radio. . ..

Dell was where he needed to be right now. Where all his listeners and friends and his family lived.

Where we used to live.

Dell Markle had come home for Christmas, and he did not intend ever to leave again. He took one last draw on the cigar, lifted an ear to the broadcast, and ground the smoke out on the heel of his boot. Time to get back at it. Dell did not want to miss his introductions to the next round of music and the sponsor's announcements.

He would not miss it for anything in the world right now.

It was late April in the following spring after the explosive return to the radio airwaves of Mr. Dell Markle and the meteoric rise from the ashes of A.M. radio station WLJH at six-seventy on the A.M. dial.

Lloyd Harbaugh parted the curtain on the front window of the office at the brick building labeled with the brand-new sign with the fancy new logo of the radio station proclaiming this to be the proud headquarters for A.M. radio station, WLJH. Lloyd smiled as he watched the prized Karmann Ghia of Mr. Dell Markle pull into his parking space. Lloyd then thought about how he still had to find the time to plant that signpost for Dell's reserved spot into the ground. It was a long, hard winter, but this was a warm spring day and the ground and the landscape around the radio station's property began to thaw out with the recent changes in the weather. Now, with some office help and some college interns working in the station's office, his schedule will loosen up considerably. Recently, his son, Mark, had left his former full-time position to work in the station now along with Dana. Things were not just looking up; they were better than any of their wildest dreams could be. All because of a letter and a return home to where they all used to live. Lloyd admired the Ghia, which Dell just picked up last week out of the paint and body shop. Dell had the

Ghia painted to its original yellow color, the rust cut out and repaired, the car's interior restored and the car's engine and mechanicals revitalized. Dell had the top down on this warm day, and his trademark cigar smoke drifted into the air. He was indeed the epitome of a "COOL DJ" just as his custom license plate proclaimed. Lloyd glanced at his wristwatch and noted that Dell was early, as he usually was, but today he was even a few minutes earlier than was his usual routine time. Within a few short minutes, Dell strode through the door, he carried his small canvas bag with his prized cans inside, and he sported new spring threads, with black dungarees, a black dungaree jacket, dark sunglasses and shiny black boots on his feet. He even had a fresh haircut and his beard trimmed. Dell Markle was looking fine today.

After the usual morning greetings, Dell, as was the usual routine, prepared two cups of coffee for Lloyd and Dell to enjoy as they went into the morning recap before the Morning with Markle show went on the air.

When the business of the day ended, Dell looked at Lloyd, pointed at the guest chair in front of the desk and asked, "Say, can I sit here for a minute? I need to tell you something before you hear it elsewhere."

Lloyd felt the rather serious tone of Dell's voice resonate throughout his body and shake his very soul.

Lloyd could not help but to think, 'Just when things were rolling so perfectly. Dell is going to be leaving us.' Lloyd tried to keep his composure, he slid forward in his chair, picked up his coffee mug, took a sip to steady his nerves and try to hide his apprehension at the foreboding words, pointed at the chair and mumbled, "Yes, of course."

Dell sat down and his words moved straight to the point, "I received a call . . . from old man Davidson . . . at the bank." Dell stopped speaking, and he studied Lloyd's face and saw that concern enveloped his face and Dell felt the need to continue to explain without further hesitation, "He invested in an A.M. station in New York City. Big boy, clear channel, fifty thousand watts."

Lloyd nodded and said, "I see, and let me guess, he offered you a job there and wants you to move the Mornings with Markle show over there?"

"Yes, but, Lloyd. . .."

Lloyd held up his hand while remaining very determined to show Dell that it was okay and to try hard to show him that the news would not tear him apart. After all, Dell had every right to move where he wanted to; WLJH was only five-hundred watts daytime and a peanut whistle at night. They had no contract. No official agreement and Dell earned this right.

"Look, no hard feelings, Dell. I know we are only a peanut whistle station that is powering up a wet noodle. Sounds like it is a dream fulfilled for you and you really should. . .."

Dell cut him off. "Lloyd, please."

It was hopeless because Lloyd was hell-bent on providing understanding to his star disc jockey, "I understand, Dell. It is. . .."

"Lloyd! Listen to me! Damn! Will you just shut up for a second! I turned him down, Lloyd."

The shock of the words caused Lloyd to shuffle

his coffee mug and knock some of the coffee over, and Dell moved quickly to pick up some papers from the desk, so they did not become coffee soaked.

"Oh, geez! I am so sorry! I hope that my reaction and clumsiness did not get coffee on those new clothes, Dell. But did you say that you turned old man Davidson down?"

"I did. I thanked him, wished him luck in duplicating what we did here, and told him that I was staying right here at WLJH. I also told him that I hoped he would still continue to sponsor the show."

Lloyd ignored the coffee puddle on his desk, pushed back into his chair, and studied Dell's face.

"What did he say?"

"He said that he was going to continue to sponsor the program and in fact, he was going to look into buying some commercial time for his other business ventures. Something about a restaurant that he is opening in Phillipsburg."

Lloyd finally forced a smile, reached into his desk drawer, shuffled around for a roll of paper towels, and began to clean up the spill.

"Why, Dell?" Lloyd asked as he cleaned up the coffee.

"Why, what?"

"I mean . . . why the hell did you turn him down?"

Dell smiled and stood up. He reached out his hand and placed it over Lloyd's hand as he stopped cleaning up the coffee spill, and Dell gently said, "Because this is where I belong and this is where I want to stay. You gave me a chance. You gave me my life back. You made the dream a reality and brought me home to where we used to live. All of us. Me, my old set of cans, my dusty old record collection, and . . . you too. Besides, Mark is learning quickly, and he is sort of my co-host now. He brings a touch of modern music, a touch of another era, and there is no way that I could ever derail the career of the heir-apparent to Mornings with Markle. Besides, he has a great sounding voice. Luckily, he inherited that from Becky and not from you."

Lloyd chuckled at the factual observation of his lack of an attractive radio voice; he nodded his head, forced back some tears, and then pointed at the rescued papers in Dell's hand.

After some composure set in, Lloyd asked, "Did they get coffee soaked?"

At first, the question puzzled Dell. He checked the papers, and after a brief inspection, he saw that only a tiny touch of coffee licked the edge of one of the papers.

"They are okay, just a touch of coffee on one edge. Here."

Dell handed the papers back to Lloyd, who waved for Dell to keep them.

"Good—they are important. Please, read them."

Dell held the papers up and when he read them, he immediately focused on the official heading of the papers. For some reason, Dell read them aloud, "Federal Communications Commission. Application for Radio Station Licensee Modification." He read a little further, then looked at Lloyd and spotted the smile on the face of his boss and what Dell felt was now his friend, too. "You are applying for more daytime and nighttime power? Another antenna? Directional at night?"

"I am. I think we have a good chance for approval, too. Maybe not clear channel, but a few watts more. We can squeeze the BCP-1 a little more, and the summer is a good time to do antenna work. Who knows, maybe this winter, we will have to melt snow off the capacity hats. As in plural."

Dell nodded and looked at his watch and suddenly realized that it was two minutes to airtime. "Oh, geez! I have to get in there. I never miss a queue. Thanks. We can talk some more later!"

Lloyd waved in the air and yelled out as Dell hustled to the studio, "Dell!"

"Yes?"

"If you need me, I am going to be out front. I have to dig a hole and cement that signpost in the ground in front of your reserved parking spot. Going to make it permanent."

Dell smiled a wide smile. He grabbed his canvas bag, mouthed a "thank you" and he disappeared into the studio. When Dell's melodious voice filled the audio monitors in the office, Lloyd dug around in a tool chest that he kept in the storage closet in the office for a pair of work gloves. He found them, he slipped them on his hands, and he suddenly and inexplicably tried to recall some words of Pastor Derrick Deacon, and the words bounced around within his mind until Lloyd managed to recall them.

"Furthermore, if you commit your life to what is good and just and kind, then surely, the Lord will show you the way to the pathway to your heart and give you joy and peace. Do not stop, dear listener, continue to charge ahead until you find your destiny and the Lord will make your life whole and bring you home!"

Lloyd smiled, and he stood up and walked slowly to the office door. He had to go to the outside tool shed and find a shovel. When he opened the door and the warm April air hit his body and the rays of sunshine beat down upon his skin and filled his eyes with glorious light, Lloyd said, "Pastor Deacon, I owe you a sincere apology. I owe you, because I think that in all of your ramblings and your many shows, you never spoke truer words than those words are. Thank you for making me into a praying man. And I am saying here and now that the first thing that I am going to pray for, come this winter, is for a little help in keeping snow off the capacity hat. Especially, if there are two antennas by then! Forty years and forty winters, I have been fiddling with those stupid knobs. . .."

THE END

Sort of a Short Two

In the Rush of the Static

This was the moment that he yearned for and waited for not only this Christmas season but also many more before this one. An old radio bought in a thrift store was the best gift that he could have ever given to his soul.

The rush of the static in the speaker was powerful, but he leaned in over the old radio and carefully tuned the tuning knob while listening to the nighttime signals. He knew that he heard it. He swore that he did. Down deep under the mud of the static, the signal was there. If only some Christmas magic could intervene and adjust the airwaves in his favor. It was just a minute or two past midnight and he swore that he had just heard a familiar voice announce the radio station's call letters and then the glorious few opening bars of the Hallelujah Chorus played out of the radio. He swore that he heard and recognized the voice of the longtime and legendary radio announcer, Mr. Dell Markle, and he jotted down the call letters of WLJH on a notepad that he kept handy in case of situations such as this.

A quick check of the internet on his smartphone told him that radio station, WLJH was located in Warren County, New Jersey, and that indeed, Mr. Markle was on the staff there and working as the lead radio announcer and on-the-air personality. He hosted a new version of his famous morning radio program, "Mornings with Markle." He kept trying to convince his mind that Warren County, New Jersey, was not that far away, especially in A.M. radio land distance from Raleigh, North Carolina.

He grew up listening to Dell Markle on the big radio station in New York City, and no one knew rock-and-roll better than he did. The man was amazed that he was still on the airwaves, or in fact, that he was back on the airwaves. He also recalled how Dell Markle hosted a Christmas program every year of continuous Christmas music that his father proudly proclaimed as, "The best Christmas radio program ever."

It was the program of choice for listening to while opening their Christmas presents while gathered around the Christmas tree, and they celebrated the holiday as a family. The static took over, and he was about to give up when he heard the faint sound of the music gradually return. The signal grew stronger and stronger. Christmas magic intervened on the airwaves. He let his hand off the tuning knob in fear of losing the perfect setting. The band changed around, the static cleared, and the signals boomed in. The speaker of the old radio filled with the resounding music.

The Hallelujah Chorus proclaimed, "Hallelujah."

The man leaned back in his chair, closed his eyes, and allowed the glory of the music to fill his heart and soul.

He returned home once more to the place where we all used to live. The place that no matter how far we wander, or how far away that we are, our hearts never leave.

Home.

It really felt great to be home.

Hallelujah.

Flash Fifteen

The Right Side of the Grass

The pub sat on the busy street corner in the old city as if it were a derelict waiting for a handout.

It was near the bus stop. On the main line.

The flagstone exterior was dirty from the bus exhaust. The door sat on an angle and faced the corner. Two stone steps to go up and a big red wooden door to enter into the pub.

The old pub had been there for years and years. An Irishman from Dublin opened it in the mid-70s. He died and his widow ran it for a long time until she sold it to another Irishman from Paterson, New Jersey. Actually, the new owner was Irish-American. Paterson is a long way from Dublin.

As far as most of the patrons and the locals knew, he still owned it.

The door swung open, and the sunlight bathed the floor of the pub.

He looked at his watch and turned around. He wanted to greet his friend because his friend was like clockwork in his timeliness. A few other bar-stool-dwellers turned around and waved, then went back to their pints, their shots, and returned to watching the dusty old television screen hanging over the bar.

Yanks, 4, Orioles, 2. Bottom of the fourth inning.

"How are ya, today, old boy?" The friend on the stool asked the new arrival. He asked, even though he already knew the answer.

"I am on the right side of the grass, so . . . I am doing okay," was the answer.

It always was his answer.

For the thirty-plus years that the friend knew him.

The sleepy bartender slid the pint glass of Guinness over and nodded.

He dropped a five-dollar bill on the bar counter, picked up the glass, took a sip, smacked his lips and asked, "What's the score?"

The curtains in the old kitchen were dusty. So was the old man's soul. The wallpaper was more yellow than it was white. It originally was white. The old man's wife picked it out, and he hung it. That was about thirty years ago.

He could recall that day as if it were yesterday, but the trouble now was recalling what actually happened yesterday.

"I don't actually know . . . have nuthin' to base it upon . . . but right now, the way that I feel . . . I think we might live too long."

The old man fiddled with the handle of his coffee mug.

He lifted his eyes to his son and said, "I have my backpack, all set to go. I figure it might be all that I need up there or wherever it is that I land. Packed my gravity glass in there. Yup . . . gonna bring my backpack."

The son smiled at the comment. He lifted his coffee mug up and took a sip.

"You're a long way off from any trips or landing anywhere, Dad."

The old man forcibly shook his head in an emphatic testimony of his disagreement with his son's statement.

"Nope, can feel it fading every day. Confusion over simple things. Everyday things. My address, my telephone number, how to turn the television set on, ya know, things like that. The doc agrees. This is one of the more rapidly progressive forms of dementia. Soon, I will not know how to do anything, where I am, or . . . who you are. Hell, I might not even know who is playing first base for the Yanks these days. Even if he is a bum. Full-blown Alzheimer's in six months. Something about the blood flow in my brain. Yet, son, promise me this. . .."

His voice choked with emotion and the words trailed off.

"Yes, Dad."

"Promise me that you will do it. Just as I asked ya to do. It is a simple thing. I have to have it."

His eyes gleamed with hints of mischief. "Yes, Dad, I will do it just as you requested."

"Good. Thank you. Be sure to give the grave workers this twenty-dollar bill for doing it. Tell 'em to have a beer on me."

The father reached into his pants, pulled out a twenty-dollar bill, and placed it on the table.

"It's gotta be this dough. I blessed it with a touch of spilled Guinness. Ya better do all of this or I will come back and haunt ya ass," the father said with a playful wink of his eye.

They finished the coffee in silence.

The funeral director tucked the backpack into the casket after the final viewing. The crew closed the lid and sealed it.

The funeral director also double-checked the arrangements with the cemetery manager. And the son, just before the pastor began the graveside service, scooted off to check with the foreman of the crew. The crew stood off to the side, waiting for the service to conclude before they finished their work.

"It is there?"

The foreman smiled, nodded, and answered, "Yup. A three-by-three section of sod. I think it is bluegrass. I placed it in the bottom of the grave myself. Spread it out all nice and flat and even."

"Thank you. Here is twenty bucks from my old man. Please, get a beer for you and your buddy here. It is on my dad to youse guys."

The foreman took the money, nodded, and stuck it in his jacket pocket.

The epitaph on the gravestone read, "I am on the right side of the grass, so . . . I am doing okay."

Flash Sixteen

A Fine Cigar

He sunk down in the chair in his living room and left out a heavy sigh. How will he tell his wife what happened? The drinking part is easy to explain. She knew he loved the Irish. Grabbing a handful of his assistant's glorious ass would not be so easy to explain.

He would polish up his resume and send out some right away. Accountants are always in demand, maybe not executive directors of accounting for worldwide corporations, but accountants in general are always in demand.

Or so he hoped.

He could explain in the job interview how he was going to rehab. That might or might not be a lie. The next few days might determine that fate.

It would not be easy.

His watch told the four o'clock in the afternoon story. His heart told him of the doom looming. Such a superb job, and he was so foolish. Another hour and his wife would be home.

He would pour three fingers of Irish in a faceted glass and try to dull the pain. The memories of that wicked hangover the day after the party were very faint now.

In retrospect, it was a fine cigar.

From what he recalled of it through the drunken haze; her ass felt as good as it looked.

The Director of Security did not even knock on his office door. He walked in and had a blank look on his face. With a mumble and a point at the desk, he motioned for the office mailroom crew to drop the boxes.

"Please, place them on the desk and the floor. Thanks."

The crew brought the empty boxes in, set them where he asked them to do so, turned, and left.

One of the crew turned and said, "Page us if you need some two-wheelers to get them to your car."

He did not answer. Unless only a nod counts for an answer.

His eyes met the director's eyes.

He only shook his head and mumbled, "Sorry. The big Japanese bosses did not accept your apology. It was an expensive cigar. You better hope her husband ain't waiting for you outside," the director said as he pointed his right thumb in the direction of the desk outside his office.

Where his, now, former assistant sat. She was not in today. She knew that the train was pulling into the station today.

"Human Resources will have some papers for you to sign. Stop by there on the way out the door. Good luck."

He stood up and nodded in understanding.

The uniformed security officer stood outside the door with his arms folded across his chest. Imposing.

The office area outside his office went silent. Only a phone or two rang here and there. No tapping on typewriters. All of his now former staff leaned in and listened to the drama unfolding.

He was getting the boot.

The disc jockey played, 'Rockin' around the Christmas tree.' He danced across the floor, a lot tipsy and very happy. He loved Christmas, and he loved this song too. He waltzed by the table full of the stuffy Japanese bosses. That one guy who looked like a frog never smiled. Mr. Naka-something-or-other.

His hazy mind could not think of his name. All he knew was that their eyes met, and that he did indeed, look like a frog. Mr. Naka-something-or-other puffed on a big cigar and frowned at him as he danced by with the Santa Claus hat on his head.

The thought ran through his head about how this clown looked like a frog and how he must hate Christmas. He plucked the cigar out of his mouth, stuck it in his mouth, and while the group of Japanese executives sat horrified at his actions, he leaned in and messed up the frog's hair while saying, "Lighten' up frog-face. Happy Christmas!"

The disc jockey stopped the music. Everyone stopped dancing except for the Director of Accounting. No more 'Rockin' around the Christmas Tree.'

For the worldwide corporation.

The Director of Security saw the horrible scene unfolding while he stood on the sidelines watching the part-goers.

He thought, 'I only have to suffer through two more of these stupid parties and then I can retire.'

How he despised the annual Christmas party.

'Bunch'a drunks.'

He grabbed the lapel microphone to his two-way radio and radioed into his officers that trouble was afoot. He raced across the dance floor. He was too late.

The Director of Accounting spotted his assistant. Her mouth was agape.

He thought, 'How her pants were tight and her breasts looked amazing in that holiday sweater. She has such a perfect ass.'

While he took a puff on the cigar, he leaned over, winked and grabbed a handful of her backside in those glorious tight pants. Secretly, he knew she loved it as she jumped and screamed.

'Damn, it was a beautiful ass.'

He knew it would be.

A corporate security officer wrapped his arms around him.

He thought, 'How this Irish whiskey generally led to nothing very good.'

He now had positive proof of that fact.

That is the way that life goes sometimes.

Two fingers in the faceted glass were not enough. He made it three. He heard the garage door open and his wife's car pull in.

Better, make it four.

In retrospect, it was a fine cigar.

Spark Six

Not-For-Profit

"Behind every not-for-profit corporation; someone is making a whole helluva lot of profit."

Flash Seventeen

Tricky Choppers

The Ferris wheel operator looked at him and blinked. He rubbed his right arm with his left hand and then scratched at an invisible itch. He then looked at the young woman standing next to the hockey player and continued to rub his arm as his eyes worked her over. He reluctantly rolled his eyes away from her magnetic tube top and then pointed his eyes in the direction of the hockey player and blinked again.

"Say again, guy? Youse want me to do what because of what?"

His eyes went back to her tube top.

He thought of his probation officer lecturing him to stay out of trouble. To top off his thoughts, this hot chick's boyfriend was huge. As in large and athletic and muscular.

She might be worth the tussle and trouble. Then again, she might not be. The guy was huge.

"Well, then at least, use some denture cement to hold your dentures in. Especially so for the upper plate. The bottom plate is tight, but there is some play on the upper plate. Are you sure that you do not want me to reline the uppers?"

The hockey player waved his hand in the air dismissively in the dentist's direction. He had spent enough dough with this white-coated thief.

Cursed hockey pucks. The impact of the blow was still fresh in his mind. Even though it had been years.

"Nah, I just suck them in tight. Suction works just fine. I don't need to spend anymore dough that I don't have. Tryin' to make the final cut here. Down to two defensemen to beat for a roster spot."

"Okay. Good luck."

It was the 1970s. Peace, love, and rock-and-roll. Tube tops, halter-tops, bell bottom dungarees, and hair dyed with flashes of lighter colors.

She wore a tube top that hugged her generous and perfect breasts like a passenger held onto the deck rail of the Titanic. A death grip on impending doom. The top was bright yellow, and you did not need much imagination to describe every detail of her breasts hidden underneath there.

She had to tug at the tube top every few seconds to make sure it was in place.

Her hair was light brown and the gold highlights dyed into the weaves of her hair flashed, "Love me" in the waning summer sunlight.

The main avenue of the carnival flickered to life in the pending evening. Reds, greens, blues, yellows and every color in between. The hockey player took her hand, and she took his.

The hockey player was in love. So were every other male and even some females at the carnival that were lucky enough to catch a glimpse of her. They all glanced at her and wished she stopped tugging so much. Just a slip.

The carnival was a traveling affair. There were

many affairs going on here and there and everywhere. Some hidden and some not.

Most of the workers of the carnival were just out of jail in the spring of this year. They needed to report to their individual probation officers at the end of this tour.

The traveling affair was making the rounds of the country. Fund raisers. Now, the Totowa, New Jersey Volunteer Fire Department reaped the rewards of one of the last trips before the summer ended. Labor Day was the breakpoint or thereabouts.

He had won her a teddy bear on the bottle toss and won her heart. At least for the rest of the night. Maybe longer. Who knows? He did not tell her that he was an ice hockey player. She commented on his muscles and athletic build.

He would pick the right time to tell her.

The hockey player caught her checking out his ass, and she caught him checking out hers too. Her hip-hugger bellbottom dungarees sure hugged.

The Ferris wheel loomed on the end of the carnival, while towering above the asphalt and the other amusements with its flashing lights of allure.

Reds, greens, blues, yellows and every color in between. The colors spun around and around in a blur and a trail of colors. A wheel of colors.

Of course, the hockey player had to rock the Ferris wheel car when the operator stopped it right at the top. That was part of the evil plan and the standard procedure for the ride operator for whenever the wheel had many pretty gals spinning around on it. The same operator who had stared at his new gal's nearly exposed chest.

She squealed and laughed in delight and begged him to stop. She forgot to tug at the top.

It was just a slip. Just enough. The hockey player was in love. Perhaps he might always be.

The sunset dipped just below the horizon. From the top of the wheel, they could see forever. Forever and then some more. At least, just beyond the edges of Route 46 below them and over towards Little Falls. Headlights were now on and they lined and defined the highway, leading the path to Willowbrook and beyond.

The colors lit the sky.

Reds, greens, blues, yellows and every color in between. Then it happened. He rocked the car, she laughed and screamed like the damsel in distress, she forgot to tug, his eyes went to her errant slip and before he could react or catch them . . . out of his mouth, they flew.

They both leaned over and watched them bounce from steel rail to steel rail. In between the colors. She completely forgot about her top.

Her breasts were magnificent. Heaven.

While she tugged at the top and hid her magnificence, he spoke softly.

"Did I tell you that I am a hockey player? My teeth had a small battle with a hockey puck a few years back. In a semi-pro league game in lower New York State. The puck won and my choppers lost."

She nodded and tugged.

"Ah, say, buddy, if I gave ya ten bucks could ya stop the wheel so I could look for my loose choppers. They are a bit tricky these days.

Should'a' went for the relining. I hope they landed on the grass and did not shatter into a million pieces."

The wheel operator looked at the hockey player as if he had two heads. Then his eyes went to her tube top.

"Did your daddy ever tell you the story about when he lost his false teeth on the Ferris wheel?" She asked their children.

"I will give you a hint . . . it was on the night when we first met!"

The children scrambled to their feet, laughed, jumped up and down, and while they were all running over to gather around their father, they all yelled in unison.

"No, we never heard that story before! Please, Daddy, please, tell us!"

She leaned in, kissed her husband's cheek, and whispered in his ear, "Leave out the tricky tube top part. I will make it worth your while."

Even after all these years, she was still heaven.

Sort of a Short Three

A Stint in Gardening

The beautiful young woman made her way across the property, while keeping her eyes focused upon the perfect location. The sun was bright and powerful, and the sunrays caused her to squint to capture the area that she had in mind.

She pushed a wheelbarrow in front of her with her gardening gloves firmly and proudly gripping the wooden handles of the wheelbarrow. While she walked to the corner of the property, far away from where her family home sat on the opposite corner of the property, she smiled. In her heart, she knew this was the perfect location. There was no question in her mind. On the edge of where the trees encroached upon the land, right next to the large rock that she played upon under the careful watch of her father. Long ago, in a time when they were both carefree, and the world seemed so light, easy, and amazing.

Once she reached the perfect location, she quickly went to work. First, she grabbed the sharp-edged spade shovel and dug the holes to the proper depth and width, then she amended the soil with fertilizers and the proper nutrients, making sure that the soil was loose and free and that the moisture levels were perfect. Finally, after a careful check of the planting holes, the young woman, carefully and painstakingly, took each of the bare-root plants, checked the roots and gently untangled them and then one-by-one, she planted them and backfilled the holes. With a sprinkling can, she gently watered each plant to give them a drink of nourishing water. While she did so, there was a barely audible prayer for magic and life and dreams that she muttered and laced with her lovely voice. The gracious voice of a gentle and gorgeous young woman. A woman full of hope and dreams, but a woman that carried an element of sadness with her.

The young woman stood back and admired her gardening work. She pushed her auburn hair away from her face and pushed her eyeglasses farther up her nose. Pushing her eyeglasses was more of a habit than it was a need.

"Perfect," she mumbled, "I just know they will grow and bloom and magic will fill our lives and my tears will dry." With a quick glance to recheck her work, she gathered up her tools and placed them into the wheelbarrow. The young woman wanted to finish her work before her father arrived home. Her plan included a surprise; in fact, it had to be the ultimate surprise. She made her way back across the property, to return her tools and to make sure there remained no evidence of her mission.

In the sun's warmth, the plants took in some water into their roots, they felt the sun, and they enjoyed the soil and the nutrients. Each of the plants happily pushed their roots deeply into the soil.

The magic began.

Short Two

The Christmas Rose

A story from the *Where We Used to Live* collection of stories

"I am about ninety-nine-point-nine percent sure that you are my future husband, but until I can confirm that fact, could I please have a half-a-pound of the oven-roasted, golden and amazing turkey breast?"

Mr. Ian Fall cautiously leaned over the delicatessen counter at the Foodworld supermarket and he gingerly peeked over the glass top of the counter. Generally, Ian was rather cautious in every aspect of his life; in love, and in his overall approach to everything. Ever since, life had thrown him so many twists and turns. It was his rule of thumb. He moved a small basket on top of the glass deli counter that was displaying croutons in order to obtain a better look at who it was that just implied marriage to him as well as ordered a half-of-a-pound of turkey breast. His partner working with the slicer next to him, Susan Beckley, chuckled at the statement and Ian's reaction. Susan had worked with Ian long enough to know that his good looks always attracted attention from the female customers and female co-workers, and she always enjoyed his shy and cautious reactions to the attention. The young man had no idea that he looked better than most Hollywood movie stars look and all he wore was a deli-counterman's work apron and a hat emblazoned with the Foodworld logo.

An elderly woman stood next to the speaker of the order and proclamation and she suppressed a chuckle while staring first at Ian's reaction, and then directing her attention to the young woman standing next to her. A young woman, who dressed in a long skirt filled with a beautiful red flower print on a black background and tied off at the waist with a wide black belt. The young woman had a black blouse on and topped it with a black shawl made of thick yarn. A hat made of the same material sat upon her head, and her auburn hair stuck out in many directions underneath the hat that she pulled down tightly upon her head. Her hair was amazing, captivating, and glorious, and while it initially felt the influence of her hat and ran in many directions, the curls eventually settled out and tumbled in graceful waves down upon her shoulders and her back. The auburn highlights of her hair reflected in the rather harsh white lights of the supermarket and broadcasted the depth of the color of the hair. The purpose of the lights was to illuminate merchandise to entice customers to purchase products; however, in this case, the light enhanced the young woman's beauty.

Ian carefully scanned the young woman and quickly determined that all of her garments appeared handmade except for the black boots on her feet. Black boots that rode up to her ankles and boots that wore a shiny black buckle upon the middle of them. The young woman was different, but she was captivating and gorgeous.

She pushed up at her black framed eyeglasses, which covered sea-green eyes. She smiled and, as she obviously enjoyed the fact that Ian studied her rather carefully, she coyly added, "Please slice it a little on the thicker side. This is my Thanksgiving dinner. I warm the turkey up, put it over toast and drown it in gravy. Canned gravy is fine for me. I have some green beans, a side of stuffing, and some cranberry sauce. The jellied kind, not the whole berry kind. Those seed thingys from the whole berries get jammed in your teeth."

Autumn opened her mouth and used her fingernail to demonstrate how she would remove the stuck seeds as everyone stared in at the scene. In doing so, Autumn revealed a perfect mouthful of perfect white teeth. She was a stunningly gorgeous young woman.

"They are a pain to dig them out of your teeth. Therefore, I used the jellied ones. My dinner is no mess, no fuss, an easy-peasy, Thanksgiving dinner."

Ian stuttered, stammered, and cleared his throat.

After a nod of his head and a few quick blinks of his eyes, Ian finally found some words.

"Ah, yes, okay, that does sound quite tasty and efficient. I agree with your decision about avoiding the whole berry cranberry sauce. Seems to be a . .

. nuisance. You have another choice to make, because we have two brands of the oven-roasted, golden turkey breast. Do you want the store-brand or the fancy national brand?"

The young woman did not hesitate in her answer and quickly said, "Oh, please, the fancy national brand. I have to think that I should only enjoy turkey breasts that are as fancy as my breasts are! When we become a couple, you will certainly agree."

She smiled again, pushed her eyeglasses up on her nose and tilted a little at her waist, and set the cloth-carrying bag that she held down on the floor as if to allow Ian a better view of her body. The bag appeared to be the product of knitting handwork too. The knitting style of the bag matched her garments, attire and bohemian style. The elderly woman laughed aloud, as did Susan.

The elderly woman entered into the conversation with an observation of the young woman's aggressive approach toward Ian. "Young lady, you should not hold back on your thoughts and speak your mind a little more."

The young woman winked at the elderly woman and leaned over toward her and whispered, "Well, wow, just look at him. I mean, he is gorgeous."

Ian ignored the conversation; he turned to open the display case and picked out the turkey breast from the other meats. His previous inclination to avoid the outward flirting of the young woman gave way to curiosity.

With the turkey breast now in hand, Ian said, "Why do you think we are going to marry or be a couple?"

The young woman screwed her mouth up like a corkscrew, stepped closer to the counter and answered, "Duh. Ah, because you are amazingly hot. In fact, you might be the hottest man that I ever laid my eyes upon and our names. Of course, being a hottie is simply a bonus because our names seal the deal."

Ian still held the turkey breast in his hand, and he narrowed his eyes in a display of profound puzzlement at her statement. The young woman pointed at Ian's store nametag and said, "Ian Fall. Deli Clerk."

Ian nodded and walked over to the slicer, loaded the turkey and adjusted the thickness knob.

"I am, Autumn Lynne Gleason. So . . . when we are married, I will be Autumn Lynne Fall. Get it! Autumn Fall. This is totally fate for us to meet. Over turkey breast. A few days before Thanksgiving. On a cold day. It is freezing outside today . . . that is why I am so bundled up and you cannot see my breasts so well."

Now the elderly woman laughed uproariously, as did Susan. Ian finally broke his stone face with a slender smile. While everyone else nodded their heads and laughed aloud, Ian retained his composure. He routinely sliced off a piece of the turkey breast, dropped it in wax paper and held it out to display to Autumn.

"Yes, I get it. Yes. Very cute. Ah, so, did I slice this turkey breast correctly for you? To the correct thickness . . . that is?"

Autumn pushed her eyeglasses back up her nose again; it seemed more as if it was a habit rather than a need. She made a passing glance at the turkey breast because her eyes remained focused upon Ian.

"Perfect! Like you are."

She anxiously scampered up to the deli counter. Autumn leaned in on the counter with her hands and asked with a newfound fervor in her voice, "Do you have a middle name, Ian?"

"Wilson. My middle name is Wilson."

Autumn leaned back and sighed. Autumn tended to be very animated in her reactions to her emotions.

"My goodness, Wilson. Ian Wilson Fall. His full name is as sexy as he is, and his voice is smoother than the finest Scotch whiskey in a glass is. Now, mind, you. You should only drink fine whiskey from a glass. Drinking it directly from a bottle is crude and rouge. Not that I am much of a Scotch whiskey drinker, that is. In fact, Scotch is not really my preference as far as whiskey goes. Since my heritage is Irish, I lean towards the Irish whiskies. However, actually and honestly, I like bubbly Moscato in a flute glass the best. It is my fave."

Autumn rapidly blinked several times while she waited for a response from Ian. From anyone.

She tended to ramble quite a bit.

No one spoke, and Ian quickly returned to his slicer. Autumn's shoulder slumped a little and her posture changed from confident to slightly meek. Susan finished slicing the elderly woman's selection of meats and Susan wrapped the cold cuts, bagged them, walked over to the counter and handed the package to the elderly woman.

Susan asked, "Will that be all for you this

afternoon?"

"Yes, thank you," the elderly woman answered while placing the package in her shopping basket. When she turned to leave, the elderly woman leaned in and whispered to Autumn, "go for him, young lady. He is worth it. I can tell. He is shy, devastatingly handsome and humble. You are gorgeous. I agree that Autumn Fall would be a wonderful name. By the way, I love Moscato in a flute glass too."

The elderly woman gently patted Autumn's arm and winked at her before she shuffled off and was on her way. Autumn smiled and nodded, and she bit her lower lip while she studied Ian. As usual, her exuberance and rambling had turned off a man. She could not help it or suppress it, because it was Autumn. She was the fidget-bottom in the church pew, she always raised the ire of the schoolteacher because she was the talker in school classrooms, and Autumn was the first one to claim a lunch time seat in the cafeteria and babble endlessly amongst her friends about every subject in the world until everyone rolled their eyes and shut her down. Autumn bit her lip harder and pushed at her eyeglasses again; she did not care because Autumn was determined to follow the elderly woman's advice.

"Here you go, Ms. Gleason. Will that be all?" Autumn looked up and reached for the package of turkey breast as Ian handed it to her over the counter.

"Thank you, Ian. Please, call me, Autumn. No, that will not be all, because I am trying to figure out how to fit you in my shopping cart, wheel you to my car, and bring you home."

Now Ian smiled widely. He shook his head and did his best to suppress a laugh. "Well, I am kinda tall for that, but thank you for the offer. Enjoy the turkey, thanks for stopping by and happy Thanksgiving."

Autumn took the package and dropped it into her shopping cart. She then picked up her carrying bag, reached into her bag, pulled out a business card, and handed it to Ian.

"Thank you. I ordered enough of the turkey breast for you to join me for Thanksgiving dinner. Here is my card. Since we will be married someday, first, you will need to know how to contact me. Bye, for now, Ian. See you very soon."

She winked, smiled, turned, and wiggled off while pushing the shopping cart along. A middle-aged man who was next in line behind Autumn turned and obviously admired her rearview while she watched her walk away. The man had obviously overheard most of the conversation.

Ian studied the card and made a careful note of the details.

"Autumn Lynne Gleason, Master Horticulturist," followed by a cell phone number and an email address.

Ian paused while studying the card and Susan, who was now slicing another order, lifted her eyes in a careful study of her co-worker's reaction. Susan was very curious to see his next move. Usually, Ian would dismiss any female advances, but Susan had a feeling that there was something very different about this vivacious and gregarious young woman. . ..

"I will take a pound of the tavern ham that is on

sale and that young woman's card, if you don't want it. She is a hottie. I might be too old for her, but I would give it my best shot, anyway," the middle-aged man said while still studying Autumn's exit out of the corner of his eye. He cleared his throat and pointed to the card in Ian's hand. Ian looked off toward where Autumn walked away, and he smiled and slipped the card into his shirt pocket under his work apron.

"A pound of the tavern ham that is on sale. Coming right up, sir." Ian slid open the glass doors of the display counter for the deli meats and pulled the ham out of the assortment. While he walked to the slicer, he spoke just loud enough for the customer and Susan to hear him.

"I am going to keep her card. I might need horticultural services, or perhaps . . . something else."

"Atta boy, Ian," Susan mumbled as she worked the slicer. "'bout time."

Mr. Ian Fall spun the key in the lock on the side door leading to his apartment on North Tenth Street in Paterson, New Jersey. The wind swirled around; it blew some leaves on the porch and chased them into corners of the old wooden structure. There was a chill in the air as the day waned, and it definitely felt as if Thanksgiving was only a few days away. It had been a long shift at the Foodworld today. His manager asked both Susan and Ian to cover some extra hours into the next shift for an employee who called out sick and another employee who was late reporting for their shift. It was very busy at the store today; Thanksgiving is a feasting-type of holiday. Right now, all Ian was thinking about right now was a hot shower, some soup in a bowl, some bread, a cup of tea and hitting the hay early. He had to be back to work at six in the morning. Honestly, he had one other thing stuck in his mind too and that was a very beautiful, but slightly aggressive young woman named Autumn Lynne Gleason. Her voice, her smile, her antics and her bold prediction for their mutual future worked at the edges of his mind ever since she showed up with her smile and her beauty at the deli counter this afternoon.

When Ian swung the door to the apartment open, he heard the landlady's door open next to him and

Mrs. Gilliam stepped out of her first-floor apartment.

"Oh, hi there, Ian. I am just checking my mail. You are late today."

Mrs. Gilliam gave Ian the once-over and then reached into her mailbox centered between the two doors to check inside. Mr. Gilliam died a few years earlier and Mrs. Gilliam was pleasant but a little bit of a busybody these days. She asked Ian many questions about his social life and always haunted him to come over to her apartment for a few drinks or tea or coffee. She was still young, her husband died young, perhaps, she was in her mid-forties and Ian was never comfortable around Mrs. Gilliam. Especially if they were alone. In fact, Ian was not comfortable being around any women. He was quiet and unassuming, and ever since things went astray for him a few years earlier when he first began at Foodworld, he was very happy to keep to within his own life and live a quiet, solitary life without much interaction with any other person. Even at work, Ian stayed quiet and to himself. He seldom spoke to or interacted with anyone else. Female or otherwise. His sole companion in his life was his pet cat, Lionel. Sharing his life and an apartment with Lionel was perfectly fine with Ian. Lionel did not need much. They crossed paths when they wanted to, shared some company when they wanted to, and went their own ways when needed. It was Ian's idea of a solid relationship.

"Hello, Mrs. Gilliam. . .."

The landlady quickly interrupted Ian. "Please, call me Vivian," she said with a tilt of her head and a flip of her hair.

Ian skipped over her suggestion, "Ah yes, well, I

had to stay late to cover a few hours of the next shift. Busy day and some employee issues. Thanksgiving and all. You know. Well, I had better get inside, the cold air is rushing in and I don't want to risk Lionel scooting out on me in this cold tonight. Good night now."

The excuse worked for an escape. Ian quickly stepped inside and closed the door behind him. He made the long climb up the wooden staircase to his apartment, the stairs and risers creaking and squeaking with his every step while signaling his arrival home to Lionel and the age of the structure. This house was old, drafty, and despite the rough and difficult edges of the old neighborhood, it did have some type of charm and character. You needed to dig hard in order to find it, but it was there. Lionel met Ian at the top of the stairs, just as he always did and after a few loud greetings of prolonged and slightly painful "Meows" that exaggerated the lateness of the hour for Ian's homecoming, it was easy to see that Lionel enjoyed the reunion. Ian was quite sure that his cat would enjoy his company more once he fed him. Lionel was angry that Ian worked late, but once he had a full belly, Ian knew that he would lighten up on his attitude.

"I know, Lionel. Sorry. I had to work late. I am heading to the kitchen right now."

Ian removed his overcoat and hat and hung them up in the coat closet at the top of the stairs. He tested the air temperature and thought that it had turned too cold inside the apartment, even for Lionel. His cat enjoyed the cold and was miserable in the heat, but this was a little too chilly. Ian fiddled with the thermostat on the living room wall in order to coax a little steam out of the basement boiler and once he adjusted the heat, he made his way to the kitchen with Lionel right on his heels and next to him. Lionel's tail was straight up, ramrod straight, and his previously angry calls now settled into a steady roll of "Thank you" off his cat tongue.

In "meows" that is. In a few short minutes, Lionel was happily burying his face in his food dish; Ian was stirring a saucepan of soup while heating a loaf of slightly stale bread to make it pliable when he reached in his shirt pocket to pull out his earbuds. He was going to listen to some music to fill out the silence and along with his earbuds, he pulled out a business card. He knew that the card was in there, he knew it the entire time, and he knew that pulling the earbuds out gave him an excuse to remove the card and study it once again. Until now, it had been careful and planned avoidance. When he removed the card and studied it, her beauty flashed before his eyes and her golden voice echoed in his ears.

Ian ran his eyes over the words of her job title.

"Master Horticulturist."

'Interesting,' Ian thought. He found the title of her position intriguing, yet carefully and purposely fitting to her image. After all, she wore that skirt with flower imprints upon it. Even more fascinating, Ian felt was the fact that the card did not list the name of a company or place of employment. 'Did she simply freelance?' Ian thought. 'In northern New Jersey? In New York City at one of the famous gardens?' Ian set the card on the counter, stuck the earbuds in his ears and dialed up his favorite music. It was going to be classic rock because he was a classic rock type of guy. Nothing in the so-called modern-day music made much sense to him, nor did it have any appeal at all. Zero appeals. He was only twenty-nine years of age, but some days, Ian felt as if he was sixty-five years old. His fingers settled upon the song, "Wond'ring Aloud," and he forced a smile because that was what he was doing and feeling too. Wondering aloud about Autumn Lynne Gleason.

The soup bubbled over into a boil and Ian lowered the flame while the music and the lyrics soothed his soul through his ears. Ian liked his soup very hot. As in boiling hot, he could not handle lukewarm or cold soup. After a few more stirs of the boiling mixture, Ian killed the flame. He carefully poured some of the boiling mixture into a waiting soup bowl and after setting the soup on the kitchen table, he plucked the bread from the oven and since it was sliced already, he spread it out on a cutting board waiting next to the soup bowl. The kitchen table was more as if it was a half-table, set in a small nook in the kitchen. Two chairs at the table, although he never had any visitors. His furnishings were sparse in the kitchen. In fact, in the entire apartment. In the living room, he had an old television set on a wooden cart that he seldom if ever turned on. He did not have any cable or internet service provider here, only an old television antenna mounted in the attic. Next to the television, Ian had a radio and stereo setup with a turntable because he loved his classic rock on vinyl. There was one easy chair in the living, an end table with an old lamp and that was it. In his bedroom, there was an end table with a lamp and another radio, a bed, and a small dresser in the corner and a soft bed on the floor for Lionel to curl up in. If Ian was at home, Lionel never went in his bed. Instead, he slept in the easy chair in the living room or he jumped up to join Ian in his bed.

Ian carefully slurped a spoonful of the hot soup and it tasted salty and good. He broke off a piece of the bread and while he chewed it, Ian watched Lionel clean his face after eating. His eyes met the card sitting on the counter and his curiosity overcame him once more. Ian stood up, picked up the card and carried it with him as he sat down at the table and continued to enjoy his meal. His eyes would not leave the card. It was a magnet. On the other hand, was the subject of the card actually the magnet? It had been years since he paid any attention to a woman. Since . . . her. . ..

Despite the attention, Ian successfully ignored the advances of the women who circled around him at the store, or on the rare occasion when he went out to enjoy a beer or catch a rock-and-roll band at The Peanut Gallery a few blocks north over in Haledon Borough. The pain from her was still too intense, too much of a hurt rather than it was a memory, and even these many years later, Ian was not ready for romance. For any female companionship. In fact, for any companionship at all. Except for Lionel. His feline friend was not needy.

Still, the card was a magnet. Ian picked up his phone and pulled the earbuds out of his ears just as his namesake sang the lyrics, "Both our hearts beating life into each other. . .." The lyrics hung in the kitchen with the scent of warm bread and the aroma of the soup. The feeling to hear her voice again and to see her was strong and powerful and as he paused over the keyboard of the smartphone and poised his finger over the dial buttons while studying Autumn's card for her telephone number,

Ian changed his mind and rather harshly set the phone aside. Another slurp or two of the soup, a mouthful of bread, and Ian watched while Lionel fled to the easy chair. His belly was full and his life was at peace. It was in a direct contrast to his companion's unease. Ian picked the phone up again, and he studied the keyboard. Texting for Ian was much easier for Ian to do as opposed to speaking. It was easy to hide behind the keyboard. He opened the texting application, dialed down to the line to enter a phone number, typed her number into the line, took a deep breath and typed a message:

Ian: Hi there. This is Mr. Ian Fall. I was looking at your business card and was curious where it is that you work? Sorry to bother you so late in the evening with such a silly question.

To Ian's surprise and shock, the phone beeped with a return text within seconds after he sent his message.

Autumn: Hi there, future husband! Finally! I am out here freezing my perfect backside off waiting for you to contact me. BTW it is not late in the evening. It is only 8:30! It is not a silly question. You had to reach out and text me with any type of excuse to text because ours is true love!

Ian stared at the screen of his smartphone because he was not quite sure what he just read. After a pause and a vain attempt at recovering from the words and their meaning, he managed to type back a reply.

Ian: What? Out where?

Autumn: I am out in front of your house. Please, Ian, let me in. Seriously, it is freezing out here.

Ian dropped his phone on the table as if it had some contagious disease. He wrung his hands through his thick black hair and held his hands on the top of his head for a second or two before mumbling, "This chick is crazy. Certifiably cuckoo-nuts."

He turned and ran down the stairs as quickly as he could, spun the multiple deadbolts on the door and swung it open. He took a deep breath as the cold air rushed in and he had to agree that Autumn was correct. It was very cold outside. Autumn stared at Ian from under her wool hat. Her hair still ran all in directions from under her hat, but it tumbled in graceful waves over her shoulders and down her back. She pushed at her eyeglasses and smiled a wide smile. Her beauty glowed in the dim light of the porch and surrounded her. Right then and there, her beauty and aura invaded Ian's soul.

"Hi there, Mr. Ian Fall, also known as my future husband. Can I come in?"

Ian nodded and smiled. He held out his hand, and she reached out and grasped it. He gently pulled her inside and closed the door behind her. He spun the multiple deadbolts and secured the door. The neighborhood was rough and difficult. Ian heard footsteps in the adjoining apartment foyer, and he knew that Mrs. Gilliam must have been peering out the front door window to see who the visitor was. Especially at this hour. Especially since, it was Ian and he never, ever, had any visitors.

Right now, Ian did not really care. He had other things on his mind.

"Wow! It smells so good in here," Autumn said while scanning the apartment. Ian still had not said a word, and he cautiously wandered behind her as she walked up the stairs while trying his best not to focus on her rear view as it loomed a few steps above him. Autumn still wore the same attire that she wore in the store this afternoon. The practical side of Ian could not help but to think that is why she was so cold. The shawl looked as it was made of heavy yarn, but he sensed that an overcoat would have made a better choice for such a cold evening. He followed Autumn into the kitchen when he saw her eyes catch the bowl of soup on the table. They wandered to the saucepan on the cooker and then to the half a loaf of bread remaining on the cutting board on the table.

"Could I please have a bowl of soup? I am starving. I did not eat anything today. I was too excited after I met you for me to eat. The soup smells intoxicating and it will help to warm me up. What kind of soup is it?"

"Vegetable. Susan, who is my deli partner, makes it daily. I bought a container yesterday. Sure, I will heat it up a little."

Autumn pulled the chair opposite of where Ian had sat and she sat down. Lionel jumped up off the chair and sauntered up to her to check out who the stranger was that just invaded their space. His space. Ian's space.

"Oh, hi there, beautiful kitty-cat. You are stunning. Like your buddy here is."

Ian stood dumbfounded, and he slowly made his way to the stove to prepare Autumn a bowl of soup. He was walking as if he was half-asleep or perhaps dreaming all of this.

Ian finally captured his words and reclaimed his voice, "That is Lionel. He does not take to strangers too well. Ah, well, we, never really have any visitors unless it is a repairman to fix something in this old apartment. It is very old and often needs repairs. Especially plumbing repairs. Lionel runs and hides from strangers."

Autumn was speaking very gently to the old cat and scratching at Lionel's face, and she leaned back in the chair and patted her lap as an invitation to the old cat. To Ian's astonishment, Lionel jumped up in her lap and curled up, and his purring was so loud that Ian felt as if the floor was vibrating from the rhythmic purr of his cat.

"Of course, he would not run and hide from me. He loves me. Lionel is very smart. Besides, he knows that I am your future wife. Cats are clairvoyant. They can see into the future and are aware of their past. I am quite sure that I knew Lionel in a past life. He loves you very much, Ian. See how he studies you for acceptance of him jumping into my lap and allowing me some snuggle time. Now, he feels as if he found another friend in this world. A familiar face," Autumn said as she blinked a number of times and pushed at her eyeglasses. Ian did not comment, but he turned the flame up under the saucepan and immediately vapors of steam emitted from above the pan.

"My goodness, Ian. The soup is hot enough. I don't want to melt my mouth. I will need it later," Autumn said with a wink.

"Oh, sorry. I like it hot. As in very hot." As soon as he said the words, Ian blushed and regretted allowing them to escape his mouth.

"I will keep that in mind, Ian."

Autumn slowly worked her shawl off her shoulders and let it drape upon the back of the chair, all without disturbing Lionel, who now seemed as he settled into a fast and sound sleep upon her lap.

"I meant the soup, Autumn. I like all my food very hot. Especially soup."

"Of course," Autumn added while adding an air of disbelief to her words and a coy smile poised on her face. "So, to answer your question, which as I mentioned was just an excuse to text me, I don't actually have a place of employment. Well, not in my chosen field, that is. Horticulture is my chosen field."

Already, Ian sensed that Autumn was going to ramble on with an answer. They had only spent a few quick minutes together, but he felt as if he already knew her very well. He continued to pour a bowl of soup for her while he listened. "I work in the women's clothing department at Stern's Department Store up in Wayne. I sorta live in Wayne. However, I am a Master Horticulturist. That is what I do. Well, sorta do. Mostly, nowadays, for now at least, I sort clothes and assist customers, but someday. . .. I am going to be a horticulturist at a major garden. When we are married."

Ian still did not say a word. He carried the bowl of soup over along with a spoon and after setting it in front of Autumn, he walked over to his chair and slowly sank down in the chair to study her. Lionel did not move a muscle, even when she shifted in her chair to move closer to the table to enjoy the soup.

Autumn giggled a bit and softly said, "He is so warm on my lap. Anyway," she picked up the spoon, dipped it in the soup, blew on the mixture, and then took a careful sample of the soup, "my boss says that I talk to the customers too much in the store. I oversell. I just can't contain enthusiasm for things. I don't buy anything there. I make most of my own clothes. Even with an employee discount. I prefer my own clothes. Store bought seems so shallow. I mean . . . even my undergarments are homemade. My breasts are rather large and heavy, and I can sew support better than I can buy it. I know all the right places to provide support."

Ian swallowed at the thought, and Autumn blinked and pushed at her eyeglasses.

"This soup is marvelous. Did you finish yours?"

Ian looked at his soup bowl and while it still had a few spoonfuls left it in, he decided that he was finished.

"Yes. The soup is wonderful. We sell out of it right away. Susan is a remarkable cook."

He pushed the bread over to Autumn, and she mumbled, "Thanks," and she took a slice. It appeared as if she was famished. They sat in silence for a few minutes while Autumn ate, and that in itself seemed to be a rarity, given her penchant to talk.

Ian broke the silence, "Did you really wait outside my apartment until I contacted you? I mean you knew that I would eventually text you? How long were you out there?"

Autumn swallowed some soup and smiled.

"Duh, Ian. Of course, I knew. We are to become husband and wife. Fate. So, yes and yes. Well, I was out there for a few hours. I found a parking space, and it was on the opposite side of the street. A neighbor came out and left, and the parking space opened up next to your house. I moved my car and kept the engine running, but your downstairs neighbor kept parting the curtain and peering out at me. I figured she was going to call the police on me, so I shut off the engine. That is why I got so cold. I am warm now. Thanks to Lionel and your soup."

She reached up and pulled her hat off, and when she did so, her hair escaped and tumbled in great waves of magical allure from underneath the wool, across her shoulders, down in front of her breasts, and Ian took a deep breath. Never had he seen such a beauty. Ian stood up and walked over and with his hands, he motioned for her to hand him her hat and she did so, while Ian gently worked the shawl away from her and lifted it off the back of the chair.

"I will hang these up for you."

Lionel stirred, and he looked up over the edge of the table and sampled the air. The soup had caught his fancy.

"He enjoys licking the bowl. That is, if you are

done. There is more on the stove if you are still hungry."

"Oh no, I am good. Thank you very much. It really hit the spot on such a chilly night. It was amazing."

She lifted the bowl off the table, set it down on the floor, and Lionel jumped off to enjoy the remnants.

"I suppose you found my address on the internet?"

Autumn spun around in her chair to face Ian and replied, "Why yes, of course. It was easy. It is not as if your name is John Smith. Or, Harry Jones. There are not too many Ian Falls in and around these parts. Maybe in Ireland, or Scotland, but not here. I did do some in-depth research on the heritage of your last name, and it is either Scottish or Irish. Your family simply dropped the M-C or the M-A-C along the way."

Ian nodded and after hanging up her garments, he stood in the living room and studied her. It was as if he was feeling his way as to what to say next.

"I guess you think it was as if I was stalking you?"

"I admit that the thought crossed my mind. Yes."

She waved her hands in the air in an effort to dismiss the thought and claim and explained as she continued to wave in the air, "It appears that way, but it was more as if it was a stakeout."

"A stakeout?" Ian asked.

"Yes. Stalking sounds illegal and harsh. A stakeout sounds better, and it is in this case, I feel that it is a more fitting description. You know . . .

as the police do. Checking out the neighborhood for the bad guys or to find clues to help the good guys. I was simply waiting for you to reach out and I was correct in my prediction."

"I see. Yes, I did reach out. However, Autumn, might I point out that you are not affiliated with the police or any other law enforcement."

Ian felt the need to confirm that fact. Despite her testimony as to working in retail, with Autumn, it seemed difficult to determine exactly what she did to earn a living.

"Ah . . . are you?"

She shook her head to indicate no and then spoke, "No. No police careers, a legal career loomed at one time, but that is a different story and a source of some background angst and ongoing pain. We can shelve that discussion for now. Anyway, I knew in my heart that you would reach out to me. I felt it in my heart. I can feel certain things. As Lionel did and I do when I knew that I know Lionel from a past life."

"You can feel certain things, huh?" Ian leaned on the wall and crossed his arms across his chest. "What do you feel right now, Autumn?"

She studied Ian very carefully; then she slowly stood up from the chair and adjusted her skirt. Her hair fell all around her, and Ian admired her allure. Her figure was amazing. The blouse hugged her perfect breasts, the skirt moved in gentle waves across her flowing hips and she bit her lower lip before answering.

"I feel as if we should kiss. I mean, I have a passing anxious thought that there were onions in the soup and I might taste and smell like onions, but you had the soup too. Right? It was vegetable soup and onions are technically vegetables." Autumn leaned forward, looked inquisitively at Ian, and asked, "Were there onions in the soup?"

Now, Ian had lost all his inhibitions. His past and the pain were now far away in the rearview mirror. This beautiful woman just magically erased everything. Autumn Lynne Gleason was irresistible.

He smiled, nodded, and said, "Yes, I think so, and yes, I had the soup too."

"Okay, good then, I guess we will be even. I would hate for our first kiss to be onion-filled on only my side. If we both ate the same thing, then we will not notice it."

Ian slowly walked over to Autumn.

While he walked, he said, "What is it that your boss told you?"

"That I talk too much and oversell things."

Ian gently reached out for her and pulled her close. Autumn willingly melted into his grasp. He tilted her chin to meet his, stared in her eyes and lost himself forever.

As their lips gently met, Ian whispered, "He may or may not be correct. I do know that this might be one way to stop you from overselling. . .."

The kiss lasted forever. They enveloped each other and while they kissed, their bodies snuggled into each other.

When the kiss finally ended, Autumn gently leaned back in Ian's arms and asked, "Do you have any tea? There is an old Irish custom that when a kiss makes a woman's toes curl and her lady bits ache, then for good luck and to ensure future kisses that are exactly the same—you are supposed to have tea."

Ian looked puzzled, but managed to answer, "Yes, I have tea. Admittedly, I am not an expert in old Irish customs because I am more Scottish than Irish, but I never heard of such a saying. Yes, indeed, I have tea. Lots of tea."

"I am pretty sure that I just made that old Irish custom up, Ian. After all, old customs need to begin somewhere. Just think that someday in the future my new custom will be old and since I am Irish and you are a little Irish too, then women with curly toes and achy lady bits due to amazing kissing will adopt the custom. Honestly, I made that custom up because I needed to come up for air because I was about to lose my soul to you. Not that I would mind losing my soul to my future husband, but right now, it might not be a convenient time to lose my soul. Anyway, I have never been kissed like that. Did you taste any onions?" Autumn playfully held her hand over her mouth and added, "I didn't. You tasted like magic. I am not sure exactly what magic tastes like, but I'm pretty sure that it tastes like. . .."

Ian smothered her mouth with his mouth once more and proved that indeed, there was one way to stop her from talking and he was going to keep testing his theory until it proved otherwise.

In fact, he planned to test it all night long.

"I must say," Susan said between wipes of her meat slicer with a cleaning rag, "you do seem particularly jovial today, Ian. You are not your usual quiet, polite, but brooding self. Has the holiday spirit finally captured you? Or perhaps, it is something else? Maybe a gorgeous but quirky young woman, who stopped in yesterday and sort of, kind of, made her attraction to you very obvious?"

Ian Fall looked up from cleaning his slicer and smiled an impish smile. He shrugged his shoulders and continued to clean the equipment. "Oh, okay, I see now, no answers even to your long-time partner of the deli slicing and crazy customer wars. Tight-lipped means one thing. A certain young woman made an impression."

Ian finished cleaning the slicer and smiled again while walking over to the sink to clean his rag. He looked over his shoulder at the front of the deli counter to check for customers, and seeing none, he turned on the sink faucet and washed out the rag.

"Well, let's just say that I am in a good mood, Susan. As you know, I am a private type of guy."

"Ah, yes, I noticed. We have been partners for seven years, Ian, and until today, I never heard you say more than seventy-three words to me in a single day and more than simply the bare minimum conversation with the customers. You are always polite . . . just the bare number of words. Today, when you saw Mr. Fleming's hockey tee shirt, you actually talked ice hockey with him! And you asked me how my husband is doing, and you even asked how my dog is feeling after his ear infection. Woaaah, Ian! This means love."

Susan playfully leaned on the slicing table, folded her hands under her chin, and fluttered her eyes in jest.

"So . . . Mr. Fall . . . who makes all the ladies, both young and old, faint at the mere sight of him, but will not give them the time of day, until maybe one woman finds out what time it is from you . . . any details?"

Ian finished cleaning out his rag, dropped it into the bleach sanitizer and wiped his hands on his apron. He seemed to be pondering his answer. Even to Susan, the only person who might receive consideration for being Ian's only friend. Not counting Lionel.

"Seventy-three words, huh? Ha! So exact. Well, I texted with Autumn last night, and well, she answered. Right away. As within seconds. And just to make it a little stranger . . . she was already there."

Susan stood up and grabbed her cleaning rag and now it was her turn to use the sink.

"Ah, I am not sure what you mean. There? Where?"

"At my apartment. I mean in front of it."

"In front of it! You mean she was waiting for you

to call her or text? Okay, a little creepy, Ian."

"Exactly. I was studying her business card and was curious where she worked, so I texted her and it turns out that she was out front of my apartment. She claimed that it was not stalking me . . . she was on a stakeout."

"Oh my, this gal is good."

Susan said with obvious admiration within her voice. She finished cleaning her rag and she, too, dropped it into the sanitizing bucket.

"Sounds like an excuse just to text her, Ian. Anyway. Okay, well, what happened next?"

Ian screwed his mouth up, took a deep breath and answered. It seemed as if he knew that he had told the story to this point, and it would be unfair to leave Susan without a few more details. However, he was going to leave some of them out and skip over them.

"That is what she said. An excuse. Anyway, she was freezing cold, so I invited her in and we shared some of your vegetable soup. It was the best, by the way."

Ian looked to Susan for a reaction, but she only nodded her head and smiled. Susan was intent on hearing all the details.

"Lionel loves her. She claims she knows him from a past life. Autumn is a little quirky."

Susan barely suppressed a burst of a laugh and mumbled, "Ya think. . .."

Ian continued, "And well, we kissed and then I must admit that I had the most wonderful evening of my life. I think that Autumn enjoyed it too."

Susan mumbled again, "I bet she did. What

woman wouldn't? Lucky gal."

Susan swallowed hard and tried hard to stop her mind from wandering too much.

"The best night of your life, huh? For some reason, I think the details of the rest of the evening are going to remain secret and unrevealed."

"Yes, they will. Let's just say that my nosey and widowed landlady, Mrs. Gilliam, might have heard some noises that will let her know once and for all that I am unavailable and immune to her continual flirting and suggestions. I am going over to her apartment for Thanksgiving tomorrow. We are going to enjoy that feast that she planned with the sliced turkey and extras. Jellied cranberry sauce only. We need to keep those seedy things from the whole berries from getting jammed in your teeth. Say, could you save me a quart of your turkey soup? I want to bring it with me."

Susan smiled and nodded, and they both noticed a regular customer approach the deli counter.

"Sure, Ian. You are going to need your protein," Susan said with a coy wink.

Ian waved in Susan's direction and said, "I have Mrs. Watson covered." He smiled widely at the customer and extended a warm greeting, "Hi there, Mrs. Watson. Happy almost Thanksgiving. The usual?"

Mrs. Watson seemed surprised at Ian's use of so many words, and she was going to take full advantage of it. After all, until now, she only ever heard the man speak ten words. She unzipped her overcoat; gently tugged at her bra straps to lift up her middle-aged breasts and batted her eyes a little. You can't blame a girl for trying. Women often only order a half-pound of whatever, just as an excuse to stop by and gawk at Mr. Ian Fall. The store manager loved the extra business. Ian was a very valuable employee. The manager should just have him stand in a corner of the store, smile, and greet the female customers.

"Oh yes, hello Ian. Nice to see you. Happy almost, whatever it was that you said. Yes, please, a half-of-a-pound of the store-brand roast beef. Sliced very thin. I must say that you are in a good mood. Something new in your life?"

Ian only smiled and repeated, "Yes, sliced very thin."

Susan carefully watched and listened to the exchange and then mumbled, "Ian is finally in love. This is going to be one helluva cool holiday season."

"I don't know how Lionel is going to react, Autumn. He does not enjoy change. He is declawed and seldom goes out unless we go to the vet. Those adventures generally do not go over too well."

Autumn stood in the center of the living room of her very small, almost tiny apartment and shook her head. She put her hands on her hips, pushed her eyeglasses up to the bridge of her nose, and sighed. Ian looked up at her while still holding the cage that contained the now loudly meowing Lionel. In his other hand, he held a litter box, Lionel's food and water dish, and under his arm, he managed to balance a half-empty bag of cat litter. Autumn had insisted that Lionel visit for Thanksgiving. She would not hear of leaving the cat home by himself.

"Oh nonsense, Ian. He loves me. How could you even think of not bringing your beloved companion to Thanksgiving dinner and a celebration of our love? As I already told you, Lionel and I have known each other for years and enjoyed many lives together. Maybe a few centuries. Don't be such a stick-in-the-mud-diddly-doo-dah. Now, let him down and open the cage."

Ian made a note of how Autumn did not offer to assist him with juggling all the various items that he was carrying. Her entire focus was on Lionel and his well-being. Ian carefully set the cage down on the floor, along with the other items, then he unlatched the cage and began to predict the outcome, "I am sure he is going to run and hide and then. . .."

Lionel scooted out of the cage and with his tail straight up in the air; he immediately scampered across the floor in order to greet Autumn. Autumn sat on the floor, oblivious to her skirt falling all around her while remaining stunningly radiant in her beauty.

"Oh, Lionel, don't worry. I promise that once we are married that he will not be such a stick-in-the-mud. It feels so nice to be out of the cage. Right? We are going to have a feast. No way will you miss out on any of it."

Lionel purred and rubbed his fur up on seemingly every part of Autumn's perfect body, and Ian suddenly felt foolish for doubting Autumn's decision and he admittedly felt a little jealous of his pet cat. He wanted some attention too.

"I guess that I was wrong," Ian mumbled, then announced, "I will be right back. I need to grab some more things from the car. I could not carry everything."

Autumn nodded and continued to direct her attention to Lionel, and Ian turned and scooted out the door of the apartment and headed into the cold air of Thanksgiving Day. The day was bright and clear and it epitomized the perfect Thanksgiving weather. Some dried leaves gently swirled at Ian's feet and they danced in a slight breeze with their crispy textures, making gentle crunching noises as they slowly made their way to some distant corner of the world and their final demise. Ian's eyes traveled around the neighborhood. This was Wayne Township. It was only a few miles north of the city of Paterson, and while this neighborhood was certainly a gigantic step up from where he lived, it was not located in the high-rent district of Wayne. Neat, but old apartments lined up in solid rows, all the front doors and small entrance porches looking the same in the complex. The on-the-street parking made it a long walk to the front doors of the residences.

Ian felt his heart beating faster as the day loomed in front of him. He hoped that what he felt was not apprehension setting in, but instead, it was simply hidden joy bursting through the armor surrounding his heart. Autumn seemed enamored with Lionel, and she hardly greeted him. While Ian reached in the backseat of the car to grab the soup and a bouquet of flowers that he bought for the dinner table, he tried to shake off his past and lose the doubts. After all, their first meeting ended in unbridled passion, and now he wondered if Autumn regretted them falling into bed so soon and making love endlessly on the first night that they ever met. Just a few nights ago, there was a flame of love burning so high, strong, and powerful that Ian felt there was no way possible for it to die. He grabbed the items, closed the car door, locked the door and made his way back up to the apartment. When he returned and walked into the apartment, he found Autumn standing in the kitchen stirring a saucepan containing some type of mixture while the pan sat on the cooker under a low flame. The mixture smelled glorious. Ian looked around the apartment for the whereabouts of Lionel and found him already snuggled up in an easy chair in the living room. He appeared as if he was already soundly sleeping.

Autumn pushed her eyeglasses up and said, "Oh, yes, he is fine, Ian. He was very tired from the journey and the excitement, and now Lionel wants to sleep to get ready to enjoy our meal. I am making rice pudding. I am so sorry, because I cannot rush into your arms and kiss you all over your face and body, but I have to stir this mixture continually, otherwise it lumps up, burns and turns into a horrible mess."

Underneath her eyeglasses, Autumn's eyes searched Ian's face and when Ian held up the bouquet of flowers, Autumn dropped the spoon in the saucepan and rushed into his arms.

"Oh my! They are gorgeous."

She plunged her lips into Ian's and kissed him until their lips swelled. Realizing that she abandoned the cantankerous mixture, she let loose from Ian's lips and rushed back to the saucepan and the cooker.

"Oh no! Your allure and the promise of passion diverted me." Autumn leaned into the saucepan and Ian smiled at the sight of her working so hard to save her pudding.

"C'mon, Autumn, you can do it. Stir, stir, stir, Autumn, frantically, stir, stir, stir!" Autumn proclaimed while feverishly working the spoon in the rice pudding mixture. She was dressed in another flowered skirt that swirled at her ankles and hugged her curves like a glove. Upon her feet, she wore homemade leather sandals and the blouse that she wore was open to just above her amazing and ample cleavage. Her body swayed and Ian watched as her breasts danced with her spoon strokes as she worked hard in order to recover the mixture. Ian now knew every inch of her glorious body, and he felt his body parts stir as he watched Autumn move as she worked.

"There is a vase above my head in the cupboard here, Ian. Please, use it to put those flowers in some water. And is that Susan's soup that you placed upon the table?" Autumn said with her back turned toward Ian.

"It is. This one is her famous turkey soup. I thought it might go well as an additional course. Susan's soups, as you already know, are amazing and besides, Lionel loves her turkey soup. It is what we have every Thanksgiving. I think he would be disappointed without it. It was what we were going to have . . . until I met you."

"Awesome," Autumn said with a smile.

Ian slipped into the kitchen and he squeezed by Autumn while she stood in front of the stove. The kitchen was tiny. There was barely enough room to go by and their bodies rubbed and touched as Ian made his way to the cupboard and then to the refrigerator to place the soup inside.

"I have a present for you too. I will give it to you just as soon as I am done with this rice pudding. While it cools, you can enjoy it."

"That is wonderful but, but you did not have to buy anything for me," Ian said, while he prepared the flowers for the vase.

Autumn once again fiddled with her eyeglasses, and said, "I did not buy your gift. You know, rice pudding does have a sizeable amount of sugar and starches, but it also has cinnamon, nutmeg, milk, and other wonderful ingredients in it. I think that I enjoy the texture the most. The eggs in there are full of protein too. When you mix them together in the heat, you can almost see the individual ingredients separate and then decide to come together. . .."

While Autumn went off on the virtues and nuances of rice pudding, Ian listened, but he allowed his eyes to wander around the apartment. There were only three rooms. A living room, with a very cool window seat that faced the main street in front of the apartment where Ian parked his car. The wooden seat of the window was chock full of flowers, some dried flowers and some live, some climbing plants and hanging baskets of assorted houseplants. Vines grew every which way, clinging to the drapes, the valance and the nooks and crannies to the windows. There was a small desk with a laptop computer upon it, with more flowers and houseplants in small jars and pots. A small television on a stand, a love seat, and the chair in which Lionel had curled up inside for his pre-meal nap. The walls were full of photography and samples of art. Photographs, both black and white and color with flowers, trees, plants, landscapes, ocean scenes, some eclectic modern art such as abstracts and nude men and women and a collection of photographs blended into one wall section that was devoted entirely to photos of cats. There was some Irish wall art, a Celtic cross, a picture of a piper, a picture of an Irish pub on a rugged street. The photograph looked as if it was taken a very long time ago, as did other captured scenes of Ireland.

Ian found it all fascinating. All around there were samples of assorted wall art, paintings, parchments of virtually every type of design and taste and subject. There was a small candle sitting on a brass dish set upon a table, and its flame danced in the draft of the apartment. It was difficult to detect, with the aroma of the rice pudding floating about the apartment, but the scent of the candle appeared to be a Christmas tree type of scent. Sampling the air, Ian thought that perhaps it was a fir tree scent. Next to the candle sitting upon the same table was a miniature ceramic fireplace, painted with Christmas decorations upon its miniature hearth and complete with a cat napping on a throw rug in front of the fire. Ian figured out that it was an incense burner. Of course, all hippies and bohemian chicks burned incense. A small knee wall separated the kitchen from the living room and entrance to the apartment and of course, more potted plants happily sat upon the ledge of the wall. There was a small pub table stuck in the corner of the kitchen with two stools. On the opposite side of the hallway, there was a closed door which Ian assumed that behind the closed door was a bathroom, and then another door at the end of the hallway which Ian assumed led to the bedroom. It was tidy and neat and very clean. Ian thought how the apartment was exactly what an Autumn Lynne Gleason residence should be like. It was perfect. There was a radio sitting on top of the small refrigerator, and Autumn had tuned the radio to a local station that was already playing Christmas and holiday music.

"Are you the artist and photographer?" Ian asked when Autumn finished explain about rice pudding.

"For some of it I am. Mostly the photography. I learned photography so I can shoot photos of plants and, tree and flowers. It was a minor in college for me. I enjoy learning many things. Did you know that your landlady's perfume smells like the ink used in one of those old mimeograph machines?" Autumn's question shook Ian back to reality.

'Wait!' Ian thought. 'Did she really just say that Mrs. Gilliam's perfume smelled like ink from a mimeograph machine? Where does she come up with these statements and observations?'

"Your photography is amazing. I want to learn more about that and the art but you diverted me with your comment about Mrs. Gilliam's perfume. I thought that Mrs. Gilliam's perfume smelled a little like turpentine," Ian pronounced. Then he added, "How on earth did you come up with a mimeograph machine? I have not been around one of them in forever."

Autumn was bringing out the profound and deep-thinking side of Ian's personality.

"My father has one in the basement of his law offices. He is an attorney. It is a very distinctive odor."

"Your father is an attorney?"

"Yes, and a big pain-in-my-ass. We are going to skip over him for now because it is Thanksgiving and I rather not dwell upon his curmudgeon attitude. But in getting back to Mrs. Gilliam, your landlady also has the hots for you." Autumn finished working the rice pudding; she shut the flame off under the saucepan and began to pour the contents into a large bowl sitting upon a trivet that had paintings of flowers upon it.

"Of course, most women, married, widowed or otherwise, have the hots for you. However, as of now and forever more . . . they are out of luck! There! Done!" Autumn set the saucepan into the sink, ran a little water into and then shut it off. "I will clean that later. Now, it is present time."

Ian stood there rather sheepishly because he was still stuck upon Mrs. Gilliam's perfume odor description. Autumn got his full attention when she reached down and undid the belt buckle of her skirt, then unbuttoned the waist button and quickly slipped out of her skirt. Without missing a beat, she unbuttoned her blouse and removed that, then picked up the garments and draped them neatly over one of the kitchen stools. She stood in her underwear and smiled widely.

After a push at her glasses, Autumn proudly proclaimed, "I am going to give you the present of me! Let's make love now, before dinner. It removes the lust and panting aspect of the day, and besides, we will fill up on food, we might need to use the bathroom for normal human bodily functions, and otherwise we might be embarrassed, and be all bloated and encumbered. Now we are light and breezy and free." She reached behind her back and unlatched her bra and let it drop to the floor, then shimmied out of her panties and Ian now was at full attention. In every way. She laughed and grabbed his hand, but she did not get very far. Ian grabbed her, kissed her, then picked her up in his powerful arms and carried her to the bedroom.

"The bedroom is this way?"

"It is."

"You know something, Autumn? When you are right, you are right. Your breasts are perfect. In fact, all of you are perfect. And right now, you are more-correct than you have ever been in your life. Is more-correct . . . proper grammar? Maybe, if it has a hyphen to join the two words?"

"Maybe, don't care, not concerned. We can look it up later. Did you know that relationships based solely upon lust eventually fail? Love needs a mixture of healthy doses of lust, but love is at its best when we mix lust with devotion, caring, tenderness, understanding, sharing, compromise, affection, and infatuation. I still think that I want to take you for a ton of test drives. Do you know what I mean, Ian? Sort of like a new car. Even a new used car. I need to know what makes you tick and how to drive you. Does that make sense? You are not answering. I think that my boss is correct. . .."

"I will never look at a turkey breast in the same way. In the slicer or out of the slicer. That was an awesome Thanksgiving dinner, Autumn. I loved the soup too. A perfect ending to the meal and no seedy things in our teeth. Might need to wait a bit and wait for the rice pudding, though," Ian leaned back on his stool and rubbed at a very full belly. He picked up a mug of beer and took a long swig.

"Told you so. Yes, best of all, no huge cleanup mess, just that saucepan with that yucky rice stuff on it, which you said that you would scrub for me." Autumn winked and picked up her wineglass and took a sip.

"I don't remember agreeing to that."

"Well, you did. I caught you at a weak moment, when you wanted to make love to me for the third time in a row and we were both lust panting, I slipped it in between pants. You know, yes, only if you clean the yucky rice stuff. I am in love but I am an opportunist too. It is an excellent strategy. And, right now, I am commando under these garments, so we can head right back to the bedroom before those annoying human bodily functions kick in."

Ian laughed and shook his head. This woman was amazing. She was a gift from Heaven and from all the stars to him. He had much to give thanks for in his life. As of three days ago, he did—that is. He reached across the table and gently motioned for Autumn's hand. Autumn gently grabbed his hand and their warmth filled each other's souls. Lionel was on the floor next to the table, happily lapping at the remnants of turkey breast mixed with turkey soup, and he was not missing a beat, even while his best friend was about to fall over the edge. Ian was not close to the edge; he was over it.

"I will clean whatever, whenever, forever. Anything for you. This Thanksgiving, I only have thanks for you and all that you are."

"And I for you, future husband."

Ian studied her, and at first, he thought he might skip over the conversation, but for some reason, the subject of her father nagged at him a little bit. Besides, Autumn did say they would skip over him *for now.* He did not want to spoil the mood of the day, but if they were going to share their bodies as they just did, then they should share all their thoughts. Thanksgiving was about giving thanks; it was about families and it was about feeling at home wherever you were celebrating the holiday. Right now, with Autumn, Ian felt at home. He was more at home now than he had been in many, many years. He felt as if this tiny apartment in Wayne, New Jersey, was where he was supposed to be. It felt like where he used to live. Besides, he knew where he stood with his family, but he was curious that other than mentioning her father was a major pain-in-the-ass, Autumn did not mention talking to or sharing the holiday with her family.

"So, Autumn, are you going to call your family to wish them a happy Thanksgiving?"

Upon hearing his words, Autumn quickly let go of

Ian's hand. She pushed at her eyeglasses, picked up her wine glass and looked over the top of her wine glass and her eyes widened. Ian wondered if he had made a mistake by bringing the subject up, but her voice was soft and gentle when she spoke.

"I had not planned on calling my mother today. Maybe next week. My father is home for the holidays and he would not be happy to hear from me. I only speak to my mother when he is not around." She swallowed hard and then went to continue to speak until Ian interrupted her.

"I am not. . .."

"Hey, I am sorry. We don't have to talk about this if you don't want to. My fault."

"No, Ian. We need to share everything. Be transparent in all we share and do. It is the only way. I now know every inch of your glorious body and you know mine. Now, we need to share our minds and our souls." A slight smile broke across her lips and her magical eyes flickered. "However, a girl needs to set priorities. Another glass of wine for me, and a beer for you."

Ian knew right then and there that she was correct when she called him her, "future husband." He was deeply in love. They were on the exact same page. All the time.

Autumn stood up and when she walked by Ian, he gently grabbed her by the wrist and she leaned his way. "Are you sure?"

"I am. Otherwise, I would tell you so, future husband. Unless I am layering my words within humor, then I mean what I say."

Ian nodded, he reached down and picked up the bowl that Lionel had licked clean and Ian walked over to the sink to rinse clean it. Lionel was back in "his" chair. Post-meal nap. A cat's life was glorious.

Ian spotted the yucky rice-caked saucepan but knew that now was not the time to tackle that task. Autumn handed him the beer and motioned him to return to his stool. Ian sat on the stool and took a long swig of the beer. Autumn tasted her wine, but it was not a long sip.

"My father and I do not speak. We have not spoken for many years. Estranged is the correct description of our relationship. I am an only child. He wanted a boy, not a girl. He is a very powerful and successful attorney representing high-powered clients and companies. He is the principal of one of the most successful law firms in New Jersey. In fact, in the entire nation, maybe the world. Who knows? Honestly, I don't care. Their New Jersey law offices take up about thirty floors of a high-rise office building in downtown Newark. They also have offices in Tampa, Florida, and in Palm Beach. My family is very wealthy. As in extremely wealthy. Untold wealth. Old money, Ian."

Ian's eyes widened, and she caught his eyes wandering the apartment and its cozy but humble and tiny surroundings. Autumn read his mind. Perfect lovers always do.

"I don't take their money, Ian. I survive on my own salary. I was supposed to follow in the law footsteps of the glorious and magnificent Alastair Timothy Gleason, as he did from my grandfather and my great-grandfather and so on and so forth. I despised law school, yet, I always loved flowers and plants and shifted gears to receive my degree from a different school, in a different state, in a different world, and I dumped the entire legal education and legacy."

Autumn rolled her eyes to emphasize her opinion of the extreme level of pompousness.

She then continued, "Oh my, what will the alumni think? What will the precious and pompous alma mater members think? I don't really care! Well, his hippie daughter, who is carefree, talks endlessly, can see things that others cannot, and believes that she lived multiple lives, has gravely disappointed the legacy of the Gleason family. He could not support my dreams and love me for what I am. Even with my mother begging him because he is an arrogant, mean, tight-lipped, stubborn and uncaring man. He never forgave me. I destroyed the legacy and apparently, our family's legacy is more important than his daughter's happiness. Happiness does not have a price tag because it resides in our hearts. I lost all my tears and my tears are dry. Therefore, I only want to stay positive and charge forward with my dreams. Now, I wish to be a horticulturist and tend to my plants, make things grow, nurture life from seeds and from infancy, instead of trampling upon it with laws and legal bullshit, and well, honestly, since about four days ago . . . marry you."

Tears filled her eyes and her hand shook as she tilted the glass of wine and took a sip. Ian reached out his hand once more across the table and after sipping the wine; she took it and gripped it while absorbing his warmth and comfort. She wiped away the tears and sheepishly forced a smile.

"I guess that tear wells refill. Please . . . tell me that you support my dreams, Ian."

"Of course, I do. Without question. With all my power and my presence. Let's make them all come true. Together, we will do just that. Nothing should stop us. Not mean or disillusioned fathers, or money or the lack thereof, or nosy landladies with stinky perfume or irate customers who requested a half-of-a-pound of ham and I sliced three-quarters-of-a-pound. Nothing."

Autumn smiled, and she lit up Ian's world.

"Now that I threw up in words across this table, please, tell me your story, Ian. Why is that sadness gone from your eyes? The sadness that I saw when I first laid my eyes upon you and lost my heart to you."

Ian did not hesitate in his answering of the question.

"Because . . . I know what my fate is now. It is to marry you. I am leaving my solitary life behind because of my love for you. I have no apprehension in saying that. None at all and it is scary and mystical and magical and glorious all at once but it is correct and true and remarkable."

Autumn smiled widely and whispered, "It is all of those things and more too."

Ian took a deep breath and upon exhale, the words burst out from his very soul, "My parents died in a car crash when I was twelve years old."

Autumn gasped at the shock of the news. She closed her free hand over her mouth and Ian grasped her hands tighter and continued to speak.

"My aunt and my uncle, my dad's brother and his sister-in-law raised me. I grew up in Paterson, only attended and graduated from the local high school and dreamed of someday opening up my own delicatessen. I still dream of my opening my own deli business. My uncle owned one. I worked with him in the deli from the day that they took me in. We lost the store when he died. A heart attack. Sudden. He was a wonderful man. I miss him every day. My aunt did her best to operate the delicatessen, but it was too much for her, her grief was profound, I was too young to understand management of a business and now, my aunt is all that I have left. I too, am an only child."

Autumn's eyes filled with tears again because the story kept growing progressively worse with each spoken word. Ian harbored such pain in his young life.

"You are glorious," Autumn mumbled.

Ian continued, "I had a high school sweetheart. We had been together since we were ten years old. She left me at the marriage altar. She was a no-show on our wedding day. Walked away, because, in the end, despite her words, she could not marry a man that only aspired to own a delicatessen."

Autumn lifted her eyeglasses and wiped at her eyes, while proclaiming, "She is a fool. What does money bring? Nothing but unhappiness. Look at my father. He is miserable in his constant quest for more and more money and power while ravaging lives along the way. Her loss. She gave up a glorious life and love and now it is mine to have and hold and cherish."

"At first, I was heartbroken. I withdrew from life. I vowed never to date another woman. I lived a solitary life. The mounted losses were too much for me to comprehend or manage. I vowed never to be close to another person other than my aunt. Of course, I have, Lionel. As of three glorious days ago, my life changed. I know why she left. Because she was meant to leave and I was meant to meet you, fall in love in three days and together, make all our wishes come true. I love you, Autumn Lynne Gleason. Can all of this happen in three days, Autumn? Can we meet and know that we are to marry and live together forever?"

Autumn rapidly nodded her head, let go of Ian's hand, quickly checked the position of her glasses, and downed the rest of her wine. Off she went on a weaving of haphazard words that are such a large part of her presence and her appeal, and Ian buckled in hard for the long haul.

"Yes, of course. I knew and now you know too. I love you too. With all my heart and soul, but you already knew that. I loved you at my first glance. This is all coming together now. Perfectly. I planted the Christmas Rose where we used to live."

"Huh? What?" Ian did not follow that statement at all.

"Helleborus Niger. The Christmas Rose. It is a very difficult plant to grow . . . borderline impossible depending upon the soil and climate. I planted ten of them in the perfect location on the family estate in Shadow Lakes. A perfect location for the plants and a perfect location for me. It is a special place with a large rock near the edge of the woods. I used to sit on the top of the rock with my father and tell him tall tales of where I will go, what I will do, the ships that I will sail upon and the countries that I will visit. It is the perfect location. At my family's home. Where I grew up. Where we used to live. Where my parents still live. Yes, it is in ultra-expensive and exclusive Shadow Lakes, New Jersey. Home to the rich and snooty. Our house has more rooms than you can ever imagine, or any reasonable family could ever occupy, but that does not matter. All that matters, is the fact that I know in my heart that those roses will bloom this Christmas. They had perfect soil, perfect light, their roots are deep in the ground now. I snuck in there when nobody was around and fertilized them. I know what to do to make them bloom. I have made great studies of those plants. In-depth, scientific studies of nutrients and root base establishment and time to bloom in certain temperatures and climates. I am correct. This Christmas is the Christmas for blooms. When they bloom, my tears will dry up, and my father will see me and love me for what I am. Moreover, we will get married. It is what I know will happen. Yes, indeed, I know. Do you believe in me, Ian? Please tell me that you do. As crazy as I sound."

Ian was breathless. He nodded his head and took a deep breath.

"Okay. I see. You do not sound crazy. Of course, I believe in you. You have all my love and support. Always. You are a genius with plants and flowers and everything. I mean, look around here—it is amazing. I can't grow weeds."

Ian tilted his head and stared at Autumn before asking, "These plants are that difficult to grow?"

"They are. The leaves are toxic too. Hence, their fortitude. That is why deer and rabbits leave them be and do not nibble on them. Our estate has lots of deer and rabbits living within the acreage. You plant them and do not disturb them."

"Ah, your father . . . how is he going to accept a lowly guy from Paterson with only a high school education who works as a deli clerk and dreams of owning his own deli someday?"

"He won't, but once the roses bloom, he will have no choice because love will finally fill his heart. I can see things, Ian. See and feel them."

"I agree with you . . . having been a witness to your abilities. Autumn, I might be wrong and you are the master horticulturist not me, but roses don't usually bloom at Christmastime, Autumn."

"Exactly. Technically, they are not part of the rose family of plants. They are in the family of Ranunculaceae plants, which are evergreens. You have to hear of the legend and the folklore behind the plant. Plants are just as people are. They have souls and lives, they touch each other, and they touch us in so many special ways. The legend is that a poor girl had no gift for the Christ child, and when she cried, the Helleborus sprouted up from her tears. They are magical. Like our love." She blinked rapidly and pushed her glasses up on her nose. She was truly irresistible. "Ian, did you watch the Thanksgiving Day Parade before you came over here?"

The odd question, even coming from Autumn, caught Ian off-guard. Her thoughts changed as if a windstorm captured them and her words followed the same. Spinning and twisting to the heavens and full of magic.

"The parade? Ah, maybe, just a little. I had it on for background noise. There are too many commercials. It is difficult to enjoy it these days."

Ian could tell by the look on his lover's face that she was winding up for a long diatribe.

"Well, welcome to capitalism, Ian. You are in retail. I am sure that a brilliant man such as you are, realizes that commercials are required. That parade is a bit on the annoying side, but it is very important to me. It is a tradition for me to watch the parade. I cannot miss it. Traditions are important to allow you to recall all the magic of your past and create fresh memories for your future. We cannot risk losing traditions because we might lose parts of our souls too. Traditions are a part of our past and of our future and our children's future. The children that we are going to have together. Anyway, when Santa Claus arrives at the end of the parade, I yell out to him what I want for Christmas. When I was a little girl, my father said that I should always do that. I still do it. It seems dumb, I know, but I can't help doing it. My father told me to do it so that Christmas dreams always come true. Dumb, yes, but life is full of dreams. What do we have if we do not have a dream? All we have is barren landscapes of drab and mundane existences without glorious trees and flowers and plants and joy and tolerance and kindness and love. That is unacceptable. Besides, if I can't tell you, my, future husband and my incredible lover, all the dumb things that I do, then who can I tell? Confession is purity to the soul. It enlightens you too."

Ian leaned back and smiled at her tale, her enthusiasm, and her following an old family tradition. It was obvious that despite the pain of the rift between them, that she loved her father very much and Ian made a vow, Christmas Roses blooming or not—that he would help to heal their relationship. Somehow.

"It is anything but dumb. It is gentle, lovely, and simple. I feel your joy and I love your tradition and agree with you about how important traditions are. Let's share each other's traditions and make new ones for all of us to share. By the way, you can tell me anything, my love. That said, you have me on the edge of my seat. What did you wish for from Santa Claus today?"

After a quick check of the position of her eyeglasses and a coy smile, Autumn said in a voice just above a whisper, "Duh, that you would propose to me on this Christmas Day. That my father tells me that he loves me and that he supports me and us and our dreams, and that the roses bloom to broadcast love. Ah, what did you think, Ian?"

"I think that you are amazing beyond words. I also know that you are commando underneath that blouse and skirt and that I don't care about normal human bodily functions that might come along because I am going to pick you up, carry you back into that bedroom and prove my love to you."

"Well, now, I must say that I don't really care about normal and potentially embarrassing human bodily functions either. That earlier statement might have been or might not have been a ploy. Whatever happens, will happen in this life and in the next one too. After we make love a few times, or more than just a few times, please don't forget that we have rice pudding to enjoy and you have a saucepan to clean. Happy Thanksgiving, Ian."

For Ian Fall, two thousand and seven hundred dollars might as well be a million dollars. It was about all he had managed to save in his life, and it was part of what he felt was now a pie-in-the-sky savings plan to put towards opening his own delicatessen some day. Yet, when he went to the bank, withdrew the money from his savings account, and then picked up Susan to bring her with him to the jewelry store; he did so with no hesitation at all. He enlisted Susan's aid in providing her opinion on the engagement ring that he had selected a few days earlier to give to Autumn on Christmas Day. It was Susan's idea to borrow a ring out of Autumn's jewelry box to assist the jeweler in the proper ring size for the engagement ring. Ian certainly could have selected a more inexpensive ring, but when he saw this ring, he knew it was perfect for Autumn. He had to buy it. The ring was a pear-shaped diamond of excellent quality, and the band had two small flowers molded on each side next to the major stone. Susan's eyes widened when she looked in at the ring in the jeweler's hand and she fervently nodded her head in agreement with Ian's selection.

"Oh yes, Ian. It is marvelous. I would not have thought of it until now, but I now know that you are a romantic . . . she is going to love it. I am very proud of you," Susan said as she gave Ian a kiss on his cheek. "Thank you for allowing me to be a part of this. Now, you need to sneak the other ring back into her jewelry box. I am sure you will find the correct time. After all, I bet the jewelry box is in her bedroom and something tells me that the two of you spend quite a bit of time in there." Susan gently gripped Ian's hand and winked while adding in a low whisper, "Autumn is such a lucky gal."

"No comment on where and how we spend our time." Ian squeezed Susan's hand tightly. "Susan, is this just a wild and crazy idea? I mean we have only known each other for such a short time." Ian ran his fingers through his hair as he struggled with his thoughts and emotions. "For just a few weeks. Am I going nuts?"

"Ha! You are not going nuts. You are madly in love. Weeks, days, years. What does it matter? You are in love and that is what counts. Sometimes, Ian, you just know. . .."

"I would like to meet your parents," Ian rather unexpectedly announced while Autumn and Ian sat on the love seat in Autumn's apartment. It was about two weeks until Christmas Day and they had just finished decorating the Christmas tree they bought earlier in the day for Autumn's apartment. The two lovers were enjoying some wine and beer while staring into the magic of the lights and ornaments of the Christmas tree.

Lionel was napping in his chair. As of late, he became grumpy when he stayed home alone. While in his cage, he even accompanied Autumn and Ian to select the Christmas tree. Autumn was resting her head upon, Ian's lap, her legs and feet were sprawled out across the love seat and dangling over the edge of the furniture.

"Correction. I need to add something to that statement. I *need* to meet as well as want to meet your parents."

"Okay, Ian, I understand. I think."

"It is only a few weeks until Christmas and I need to meet your parents, but I especially need to speak to your father. Alone. Can you arrange the time and meeting?"

Autumn turned her head and looked up at Ian. The boldness in his voice and statement had a tremendous appeal.

"Are you asking my father for permission to marry me? Soooo . . . sexy. Aww . . . Ian, you are such a romantic. Such a traditionalist too. You feel the need to ask my father for permission to marry me. You are so amazing in every way." Autumn motioned Ian to lean down for a kiss and he did so. Her breathless rambling did not allow Ian for any words between her words; therefore, Ian waited and patiently listened.

After kissing, Autumn shared her honest feelings, "I need to be honest—that will not go over too well. He is not a jolly, happy soul with a corncob pipe and a button nose. This time of the year, especially makes him a super-grump. He makes Ebenezer Scrooge look like he was not a half-bad kind of guy. My father is as if he is a thorn from a rose bush that just became stuck in your ass when you leaned over to smell the roses. He manages to spoil life and times. Honestly, Ian, I am not sure that I can arrange a meeting. I need to go through my mother and she will want to know the reasons why I am suddenly bold enough to return home and visit and potentially speak with my father. Why do you need to meet? Is it for asking permission to marry me? Sorry, I already asked you that question."

"One, you ask too many questions, and two, don't we need to be there for Christmas, anyway? I need to meet with your father and let's leave it at that. I have some things that I need to say and need to discuss with him. And of course, meet your mom too."

Autumn sat up and spun around to jump into Ian's lap. She draped her arms around his neck and pulled him in for another kiss.

After leaving Ian rather breathless from the kiss, Autumn asked, "Did you buy a ring for me yet?"

She blinked rapidly underneath her eyeglasses while awaiting a response.

"Three . . . you ask too many questions."

"That was already the number one item on your list. You cannot reuse numbers in a listing game. Even to emphasize a point."

"Where do you come up with these mysterious rules?"

Autumn pushed at her eyeglasses and rolled her eyes, while adding to her golden voice, an inflection of faux shock, "Duh, everyone knows that, Ian. Everyone. . .."

Ian gently knocked on the large oak door at the end of a long and somewhat dark hallway. There was one window in the hallway but since it was an overcast day outside with a light snow falling, very little natural light entered the hallway. Ian's phone buzzed with a text and Ian pulled it from his pocket and upon reading the words, he forced a smile.

Despite the tenseness of the moment. . ..

Autumn: Remember, he is not a jolly, happy soul with a corncob pipe and a button nose. I am with you and I love you.

Ian typed out a response.

Ian: Snowmen eventually melt and the ice in their hearts turns into gentle and life-sustaining water. I love you too.

Ian adjusted the volume on his phone to silence any calls or texts and tucked it away in his suit jacket pocket.

It was a Saturday, now only four days until Christmas, and Autumn's mother called her daughter earlier in the day and reported that her father had agreed to meet them today. Actually, he specifically said that he would meet with Ian, but her mother carefully worded the facts that he did not mention meeting with his daughter. Ian would not forget the pain of the fact that Mr. Gleason would not meet with his only child on his precious Autumn's face, and now, he carried that vision with him as he knocked on the closed door.

Autumn's mother, Mrs. Lucille Gleason, was a charmer; Ian instantly fell in love with her kindness, her joy at her daughter and her enthusiasm at what she knew in her heart that the two young lovers felt for each other and what they planned for their futures together. Mrs. Gleason was stunningly beautiful, with a perfect figure, many of the same facial features as her daughter had; the sharing of beauty between mother and daughter was glorious. Even Mrs. Gleason's auburn hair with some licks of gray, tumbled in the same graceful waves as her daughter's hair did. It was easy to see where Autumn obtained her own beauty from as well as her kindness and joy at everything in life. Mrs. Gleason was a free sprit and despite her wealth and glamorous lifestyle, Ian instantly recognized and admired that she retained humbleness in her soul. She smiled easily, laughed easily, and radiated kindness and joy, and Ian felt the bond between them. Yet, Ian could read the pain that the split between daughter and father caused for Mrs. Gleason. Ian suspected that in her younger days, Mrs. Lucille Gleason had the same bohemian tendencies as her daughter now possessed, and perhaps, somewhere deep inside her, she still had them.

The three of them had shared a wonderful conversation and a few cocktails, and Ian had a beer until an attendant gently announced the fact that Mr. Gleason had called to report that he now had time to meet with Ian. Yes, the Gleason's household had kitchen staff, attendants, a driver and a full housekeeping staff. Autumn warned him of their wealth, it was just a little more than he could ever have imagined. Ian was a long way from north Paterson, New Jersey. Farther than his wildest dreams could envision him to be. When Autumn had told Ian that the family house was a mansion, she had not understated the description. Ian had only seen such homes on television or in books or in his dreams. It was tucked away on a winding dead-end street in the exclusive and secretive community of Shadow Lakes, New Jersey and the home sat at least a half of a mile back from the street in a wooded lot nestled between copses of softwood trees, evergreens and hardwoods. Ian did not see very much of the home, but what he could see was beyond amazing. The entrance foyer alone with its elegant chandelier and ten-foot-high Christmas tree was stunning. The living room where the three of them had enjoyed an initial meeting, conversation, snacks and drinks, had vaulted ceilings, and it fit an even larger Christmas tree than the tree in the foyer. Ian could not help but notice the décor and the size of the room. The living room was five times larger than his entire apartment was.

Now, Ian was ready to change his life forever. He

was ready to do and to say anything to take the pain away from Autumn.

He swallowed hard and since there was no answer to his first knock, he gently tapped on the door once more.

This time, a deep male voice from within the room and behind the door said, "Come in. The door is open."

Ian spun the doorknob, opened the door, and somewhat proudly stepped into a large, dark room, with plush deep pile dark brown carpet and dark woodwork and finishes. One wall of the room had many rows of bookcases mounted upon it, and another wall was full of oil paintings of various landscape scenes and some depictions of stoic and silent looking buildings set in cityscapes. The room had a dark and ominous vibe. A large oak desk sat on one end of the room, in front of a large window, from which through it, Ian could see a large patio and what seemed as if it were miles and miles of turf and landscape. A landscape with a gentle covering of Christmas white. A landscape that contained ten very special plants within its confines. Plants of which so many wonderful hopes ride upon this Christmas season.

There was a brown leather sofa and two matching chairs, some tables and end tables and floor lamps glowing in the dark afternoon. Ian could not help but think how everything was so dark inside this room. A room, which could easily fit the entire interior of Autumn's tiny apartment inside of it and have some room to swallow up a portion of Ian's apartment too. . ..

Perhaps the most striking feature of the room, which Ian now surmised was Mr. Gleason's office, was a large wet bar tucked along one rear wall of the room.

A tall and thin man stood in front of the wet bar. He kept his back turned to Ian and the soft glow of the lights of the bar cast a gentle glow around his body.

"Whiskey, Mr. Fall? I framed those words as a question, not a statement." Mr. Gleason's voice was deep, resonant, and powerful. Ian could only imagine how he utilized his voice for strategic use in courtrooms, and to intimidate opponents, and to plow over obstacles. Ian was not even sure how often that Mr. Gleason went to court. Autumn only told Ian that he was the lead attorney for his law firm and that they represented corporations. In addition, Ian knew nothing about law, unless watching television shows about law and order counted.

After a pause, Ian cleared his throat and answered, "Thank you, for the offer, sir. Honestly, I prefer beer. I seldom drink whiskey."

Mr. Gleason slowly turned to face Ian and their eyes met. He wore an immaculate black suit, which was obviously custom-fitted and tailored, a white shirt and a black necktie with silver stripes. He was an exceedingly handsome man, with a closely trimmed salt and pepper beard and facial hair, and the hair on his head, which was also salt and pepper in color, he wore neatly cut and immaculately combed. Nothing was out of place on this man, and suddenly, Ian felt that his old, department-store-bought suit of many years (his only suit) was woefully inadequate. He tugged at his necktie to loosen it, and Mr. Gleason raked Ian over with his eyes.

Mr. Gleason held an empty facet-cut clear whiskey glass in his hand and as he paused in front of Ian, once more, his deep voice resonated across the room, "Mr. Fall, you have two choices here. Irish whiskey or Scotch. Please do not mention beer again or ask if I have bourbon here. Irish or Scotch whiskey, Mr. Fall?"

"Irish, sir. Jameson, if you have it. Please. Neat. No ice."

Mr. Gleason nodded, turned back to the wet bar and reached within the confines of the shelves and picked out a whiskey decanter.

While he poured a glass of the whiskey that was in the decanter, Mr. Gleason spoke, "Of course, I have Jameson. Excellent choice. Nothing wrong with Jameson. It is as fine an Irish whiskey as any other Irish whiskey is. Cost and price do not always define things. From your facial features and stature, I detect some Irish within you, Mr. Fall. At least, a touch. Perhaps, mixed with Scottish. I suspect your family, somewhere along the way, lost the m-c or the m-a-c in the prefix of your last name."

Ian almost smiled as he recalled Autumn's similar comments about his heritage. Father and daughter were the same in so many ways. He had to repair this relationship. He just had to do it.

"Sit, Mr. Fall. In one of the brown chairs. Use the coaster upon the end table for the whiskey glass. That table costs more than you earn in salary in an entire year."

His words were full of requests rather than invitations. This man always got his way, or at least, what he perceived to be his way.

Ian wobbled out a weakly delivered, "Thank you,"

and while he slowly sunk into one of the chairs, he immediately sucked at his inners in an effort to gain strength. His neck was wet with perspiration, and now, he felt as if he really needed a sip of that whiskey. Mr. Gleason walked over to where Ian sat. He handed Ian the glass of whiskey and then selected a chair positioned opposite from where Ian sat and he too, sat down in the chair. His eyes studied Ian and there were a few seconds of a rather awkward silence. Ian stared back and he, too, studied Mr. Gleason.

Finally, after the stare down, Mr. Gleason lifted his glass in the air and spoke, "My father always promoted toasting when you shared good whiskey, even when facing opponents and adversaries, and I would never disregard his advice, therefore, slainte, Mr. Fall."

Ian lifted his glass and gathered a few words more than what Mr. Gleason expected from deep within his own heritage and answered the toast with, "Slainte mhaith."

Mr. Gleason's eyes burned deeply into Ian's as the two men lifted their glasses and each took a taste of the whiskey and after doing so, they each set the glasses upon coasters on the end tables.

"Slightly impressive, Mr. Fall. You know some Gaelic. Unless my daughter coached you on that response, then my initial inklings of your heritage were correct. Thank you for the well wishes to my health. I already conveyed my wishes to you . . . therefore . . . let us not dwell upon frivolity and get right to the point of this meeting. Despite the season of holidays and of merriment, my workload does not cease. I am an exceedingly busy man, even on a Saturday afternoon, a few short days before Christmas. My time is valuable, and you, Mr. Fall, are encroaching upon my time."

Ian felt Mr. Gleason's rudeness and abruptness empower his own soul a little more.

Ian's words came rather easily as he felt the burn of the whiskey down his throat and its slow warming of his inners, "Okay, fair enough, Mr. Gleason. First off, since you neglected to extend any gentlemanly greetings at all, then I will. Good afternoon, sir. I am Ian Wilson Fall. It is my pleasure to meet you and thank you for taking the time to meet me this afternoon. Second . . . I did not realize that we are adversaries, Mr. Gleason."

"We are. What do you want me to do? Roll out a red carpet and bow to you? Gentlemanly greetings, Mr. Fall? I do not think so, because it is not my pleasure to meet you. I offered you Irish whiskey and made time for you, and for that, you should be thankful. I know why you are here. You have come here, to spout some foolishness in a veiled request of perceived honor to ask my permission to marry my flighty daughter. A young woman that neglects all responsibilities, all family commitments, as well as a legacy of honored family heritage. She tosses her legacy aside and wastes it all in favor of some foolishness of dancing amongst plants, and flowers, and trees and spouting bullshit of living past lives and other silly nonsense."

"Autumn is not flighty, Mr. Gleason. She is brilliant."

Mr. Gleason fiercely grabbed his glass off the end table and his temples pounded with tension. He tilted the glass over and downed the remaining whiskey in one shot, and he swallowed hard.

"And that, Mr. Fall, is a highly accurate statement and the root of the matter. Refill, Mr. Fall?"

It was now a display of Irish whiskey-induced testosterone and Ian grabbed his glass, tilted it and downed his in one shot too.

"Thank you, sir," Ian held the glasses out and Mr. Gleason stood, took the glass as well as his empty glass and slowly walked over the wet bar to refill their glasses.

With his back turned to Ian, Mr. Gleason spoke, "Autumn is brilliant. I almost wished that she was not, but sadly, she is. Autumn excelled in every education level since she could barely walk. The sky was not even the limit. Her intelligence has no limits, and that fact only adds to the tragedy of the situation. She had a pearl inside of an oyster and she chose to toss it aside for foolishness. Our Gleason legacy and our empire were all hers to hold, to perpetuate and to embrace. However, Autumn is prone to impulse and silliness and foolishness and a warped sense of reality, and that is her downfall."

"In your opinion, sir. In your opinion, Autumn tossed it aside, and that was her downfall. It seems to me that you disregard all opinions in the world, except for your own. Your own happiness means something in this world, sir. It is not always about success, money, and prestige. Sometimes, it is about the happiness within your own soul. As you correctly stated about the whiskey, it is not always about price and cost. Can you put a price on happiness, Mr. Gleason? I do not think so. Yet, it defines us and molds us and shapes us."

Mr. Gleason rather forcibly poured the refills and slammed the cap on the whiskey decanter. He picked up the two glasses and without speaking a single word, he walked over to where the chairs sat upon the plush and deep pile carpet. While remaining silent, Mr. Gleason handed the whiskey glass off to a seated Ian who said, "Thank you" and then Mr. Gleason sat down in the same chair opposite Ian.

"You are quite the powerful speaker, Mr. Fall. Strategically, utilizing my own words and meaning behind them in an attack against my position. Perhaps, I underestimated your intelligence level. I should commemorate the next sip of this fine whiskey in your honor for scoring a point or two against me, however, honestly, I will not. A seasoned attorney, capable of a vast vocabulary and you managed a slight best of me, with your, ah, ah, forgive me but your level of education, Mr. Fall." Ian took a sip of the whiskey and somehow managed to contain his anger and emotions at the pompousness of Mr. Gleason. In his mind, he recalled that Autumn had warned him. . ..

"High school. Only high school. I am . . . very well read, though. I read a great deal. I am what I am. A poor kid from north Paterson, New Jersey. A city kid. Nothing special. Hardworking, nose to the grindstone. All I am is what I am."

"Interesting . . . and your occupation, Mr. Fall?"

'Here it comes. He is firing torpedoes broadside and hitting with every one of them,' Ian thought. Yet, honesty pervaded his soul, and he was going to answer honestly.

"I am a deli clerk at the Foodworld supermarket in Haledon. It is a union position. It provides great benefits and a pension too. Not many places provide pensions these days. My parents died in a car crash when I was twelve years old and my father's brother and my aunt took me in and raised me from there. I worked in my uncle's deli until he passed away suddenly and we lost the business. Someday . . ." Ian paused and collected his thoughts and his emotions, "I will own my own delicatessen and follow my own dreams."

Mr. Gleason blinked a few times at the testimony and the truth of Ian's pain, but other than a few blinks of his eyes, Mr. Gleason did not overly react; instead, he slowly lifted his whiskey glass to his lips and took a long sip of the whiskey.

"You have known my daughter for how long?"

"Since a few days before Thanksgiving, sir."

"This Thanksgiving?"

"Correct. Yes. This Thanksgiving."

"And, you already know that you want to marry her?"

"I do. Some things are written in the wind, in the stars, and in the heavens and are unalterable. I love her with all my heart and soul, sir."

Mr. Gleason took another long sip, and then he swirled the remaining whiskey around inside the glass. "You, Mr. Fall, are a hopeless dreamer as much as my daughter is. Let us please be honest. We are both men and we can be open and honest. My daughter is very beautiful. Her female figure is captivating and enticing. I am sure, even though the thought of it makes me cringe—that you are very well associated with her allure and her captivation, and that you know her . . . well. Lust often hides within the waves of what we perceive to be love, Mr. Fall. I was young once too and fell for the allures of a beautiful woman. You have met

Mrs. Gleason. Since before this Thanksgiving, Mr. Fall, and you now are sure that you want to spend a lifetime with my daughter. Come now, please, don't be a fool. Look around here at the opulence and the wealth. How could you make her happy on a deli clerk's wages? My goodness. Such foolishness."

He lifted his eyes to Ian for an answer, but Ian did not take the bait.

"And did you earn it all on your own? Or did your family's success hand on down to you from generation from generation?"

"Bold questions, Mr. Fall. You have some courage. I had to perpetuate it. In fact, I grew the business into a mega-empire. Which is what Autumn should be doing."

"You did, and congrats on doing so, but not all of us are so lucky to have such a glorious head start with silver spoons jammed in our mouths."

Ian's words angered Mr. Gleason, and he glared at Ian over the top of his glass. He downed the rest of the whiskey and poised with the glass in his hands, while carefully listening to Ian's next words.

Ian recalled Autumn's own words and decided to use them now, "It is love, sir. Not lust. Love needs a mixture of healthy doses of lust, but love is at its best when we mix lust with devotion, caring, tenderness, understanding, sharing, compromise, affection, and infatuation. Your daughter is gorgeous inside and outside, but you cannot measure the love in her heart because it is not measurable. Her love for me, for her mother, for . . . you. I wish you could put aside your anger and your hurt, and your bitterness, and your bias and see her as I see her. As the entire world sees her. I am not a fool, nor a dreamer. Even after only knowing each other for such a short time, I know that we are meant to be one forever. I know my heart and I know your daughter's heart too."

Ian reached for his glass, took a long sip, and then slowly and gracefully replaced the glass on the coaster. He was now feeling the influence of the whiskey and his inhibitions were loose. Perhaps, in retrospect, they were gone all together.

"How many men did Autumn ever bring home to meet you and her mother?" Ian asked without knowing the answer. The truth was, they had never discussed her past, they had discussed his past, and she knew of his past love and his failure at the wedding altar, but never Autumn's past loves or lovers. He knew when they first made love that she was not a virgin, but her past was not a concern to him. The past was the past and all he could see with Autumn was the future. Somehow, Ian was confident in the answer.

Mr. Gleason reluctantly seemed to admit, "None. Ever. You are the first one."

"Exactly. And, I assure you that I am the last. From the first moment that we ever met, Autumn, called me her future husband. Autumn has a plan. She planted with great skill, research, and time, ten plants somewhere on this property. I do not know where. Only Autumn knows. She says they are planted in the perfect location. A plant . . . Helleborus Niger. The Christmas Rose. I know nothing about plants, but you can research it. Something about legends, and tears of a woman who had no gift for Christ at his birth, and her tears caused this plant to bloom. Autumn often rambles with her words and thoughts, and that is part of her magic and her love. Despite the weather, these special plants bloom at Christmastime. Her love is in these plants, her skill, her knowledge, her faith, and to her, they represent her love for you. Apparently, these plants are amongst the most difficult plants to grow and force to bloom. Autumn swears that these plants will bloom on Christmas Day and they are an expression of the healing of your relationship and are a profound display of her love. She wants to return home to where she used to live. Inside of your heart and with your love. I believe in her with all my heart and soul. I pray and wish with all of my being that you would too. Not everything has a price tag, Mr. Gleason, and love certainly has none."

Ian lifted his eyes and looked at Mr. Gleason. The two men stared long and hard at each other, and words could never convey their inner thoughts.

"Please, sir, I want to ask your permission to marry your daughter."

Mr. Gleason intently stared at Ian Fall. His dark eyes glowed and his lips quivered. He was deep in thought, and it was easy to see that Ian had hit a nerve. Yet, his bitterness remained.

"I refuse to give it. If you have your sights set on an easy life by marrying into the Gleason family, well, you are sadly mistaken. This conversation is over, Mr. Fall. I have no more time to give you. Especially when it is foolish drivel about love at first sight and fantasy about mysterious blooming Christmas plants that we are debating. Good afternoon."

The silence in the air at the bite of the words caused a long pause in their individual worlds.

Finally, Ian nodded; he downed the rest of his whiskey and smacked his lips at the warmth and the bite of the whiskey. On the other hand, perhaps, it was the words of Mr. Gleason that bit hardest. He stood up and went to hand the empty glass to Mr. Gleason, who waved his hand while simultaneously hiding his eyes from Ian.

"Leave it. There is the door. Good afternoon, Mr. Fall."

Ian nodded; he left the glass on the coaster and took a few steps.

He turned to Mr. Gleason and spoke in a low whisper, "Sometimes, you need to share the joy of Christmas with others and believe in more than the almighty dollar. You need to understand and believe in the message, Mr. Gleason. After all, sir, look around. By your own testimony, you have everything. However, do you have happiness? Someday, we will all be dust, Mr. Gleason. What matters the most is whom we loved, how we loved, and how we touched each other. Autumn loves you and when it is all over for us in this world, love is what Christmas and life is really all about."

"Good afternoon, Mr. Ian Wilson Fall."

Ian walked out of the room, slowly turned the doorknob, opened the door, closed the door behind him, and walked out to the rest of his life. Mr. Gleason lifted his glass from the table; he turned it over repeatedly in his hands and then stared at it. He walked over to the wet bar, grabbed the decanter and refilled the glass. He poured the whiskey until it was four fingers deep in the glass.

Mr. Gleason took a long sip.

The whiskey burned all the way down.

The level of the burn was immeasurable.

Christmas Day broke clear and bright, but very cold. The weather reporter's prediction was for the temperature to reach only into the upper teens. The snowfall of the last few days remained on the ground.

A frozen blanket of white purity on a weary world.

Mr. Alastair Timothy Gleason swirled some Irish whiskey around in a glass while he stared out the window of his office at the snow-covered landscape of his estate. It was early morning, but Mr. Gleason did not care because he had been up most of the evening and early morning, anyway. Sleep never arrived for him. He and his wife had attended Christmas Eve Mass at their Catholic Church, and upon returning home they had exchanged a few gifts and his wife had retired to their bedroom. Mr. Gleason felt her pain, and he deeply loved his wife, but Christmastime or not, he had ignored her desperate pleas for him to reconcile with their daughter. Now, with the love and engagement of Ian Fall and Autumn Lynne Gleason looming, Mr. Gleason felt the pain of the estrangement even more.

He already had consumed his morning coffee, and now, despite the early hour of the day, he was switching over to consuming Irish whiskey. Christmas dinner was at four in the afternoon. Roast turkey with all the usual side dishes and mince pie for dessert. By then, he should be good and numb from the whiskey. Mrs. Gleason and Mr. Gleason were the only diners. Ever since his visit with Mr. Ian Wilson Fall, his soul remained highly disturbed. He had underestimated the young man. Only a high school education, but it was readily apparent that the young man was very intelligent, and that he deeply loved his daughter. From his years of attorney work, debates, and courtroom battles and maneuvering, Mr. Gleason knew true and heartfelt testimony when he heard it and Ian's words were true and heartfelt. Could it be Fate? True love? Fantasy? Foolishness? Usually, Mr. Gleason was so precise, so exact and he was never prone to wandering. Yet right now, Ian's words ate away at his soul. The layers upon layers of his poignant words gnawed at his being and now, since their meeting, they haunted him both day and night. He recalled every word of their conversation.

"Sometimes, you need to share the joy of Christmas with others and believe in more than the almighty dollar. You need to understand and believe in the message, Mr. Gleason. After all, sir, look around. By your own testimony, you have everything. However, do you have happiness? Someday, we will all be dust, Mr. Gleason. What matters the most is whom we loved, how we loved, and how we touched each other. Autumn loves you and when it is all over for us in this world, love is what Christmas and life is really all about."

Mr. Gleason took another sip of the whiskey and he sighed while recalling another round of words from Mr. Ian Fall.

"I am what I am. A kid from north Paterson, New Jersey. A city kid. Nothing special. Hardworking, nose to the grindstone. All I am is what I am."

He parted the curtain in the office window while his eyes traveled over the landscape and more words of Ian Fall entered the dark recesses of his mind.

"She planted with great skill, research, and time, ten plants somewhere on this property. I do not know where. Only Autumn knows. Apparently, these plants are amongst the most difficult plants to grow and force to bloom. Autumn swears that these plants will bloom on Christmas Day and they are an expression of the healing of your relationship and are a profound display of her love. She wants to return home to where she used to live. Inside of your heart and with your love."

Mr. Gleason had a sudden thought. He set the whiskey down upon a coaster on his desk and hurried out of the office, down the long, dark hallway and into the expansive foyer of the mansion. He stomped over to the hallway closet, pulled his overcoat out of the depths of the closet as well as his hat, and donned the attire. The snow was not deep, only four inches or thereabouts, but he also dug out his rubber overshoes and slipped them on over his dress shoes. He checked his overcoat pockets for his sunglasses and when he found them; he slipped them on over his eyes. The sun reflecting off the snow would be brilliant this morning.

Ashley Wilkins was the housekeeper on duty today and she appeared in the foyer. She had been preparing the dinner table in the adjacent dining room, when she heard Mr. Gleason in the closet.

"Going out, Mr. Gleason? Should we warm up the car?"

"No, thank you, Ashley. I am walking on the property. I need some fresh air."

"I understand, sir. It is a lovely Christmas Day, but very cold out there. Please, make sure you bundle up tightly. If you need something, please let me know."

"I will. Yes, indeed . . . cold day . . . thank you."

He opened the door and walked out into the cold air. It was very cold outside, but Mr. Gleason felt as if it was also very cold inside too. Particularly inside his own heart. While he made his way across the property and stepped into the cold, frozen snow, his mind raced with many thoughts. He had researched the plants that Ian told him about and even though this was science; his analytical and legal mind found it very difficult to believe that plants could bloom with flowers in this cold, snow, and ice. Nonetheless, that they would bloom in and around Christmas Day. Yet, he trekked on and while performing some research; he did learn a little bit of knowledge about where these particular plants grow the best. In his heart, he knew the location on the estate that Autumn had planted these special plants. There was no question that she would definitely choose to plant them in this spot. Next to the large rock. On the edge of the woods. Where the two of them shared so many memories. Where they shared joy. Here. Where they all used to live. Where she grew up.

He made his way along and, in some areas; the snow was a little deeper. It managed to ride over his overshoes, and he felt the cold infiltrate his socks and lick at his feet. He did not care. The effects of the whiskey still coursed through his veins, yet the liquid courage gave him no warmth. He stopped a few feet away from the large rock. It was snow-covered in its various nooks and crannies, but it stood stoically and somewhat sadly while echoing reminders of Autumn's sweet voice and of his voice too. He blinked because he could see the sunlight in her auburn hair and his eyes sparkling with magic as she rambled on and on, talking endlessly in circles about every subject on earth as only she can do.

He drove his hands deeper into the pockets of this overcoat as he recalled Ian's words, "Autumn often rambles with her words and thoughts and that is part of her magic and her love."

Mr. Gleason could not suppress his smile because he agreed with that statement. Underneath his sunglasses, he narrowed his eyes, took a few steps closer, and he carefully studied the edges of the tree line of the woods. The wind blew with a strategic gust, it shook snow loose from the tree limbs, and the dry powdery snow danced in the air and stung the face of Mr. Gleason. His eyes widened when he spotted what he thought were flowers on green vines nestled in the snow. He tore off his sunglasses and ran to the spot. Lined up in neat rows, near the side of the rock, and along the edges of the woods were many green plants.

'Evergreens of some sort,' thought Mr. Gleason.

They did not really look like the pictures of the plants on the internet did. These plants were different. Some of the green foliage of the leaves ended in bright white flowers, with pale and delicate yellow wisps of stems inside of the blooms. He dropped to his knees in the snow and gently cupped the star-like blooms in his hands and felt the warmth of the tears running down his face.

"Autumn swears that these plants will bloom on Christmas Day and they are an expression of the healing of your relationship and are a profound display of her love. She wants to return home to where she used to live. Inside of your heart and with your love."

Mr. Gleason stood, wiped the snow from his knees and wiped at the flood of tears running down his face. It felt so good to cry. To release all that bitterness. His cold heart melted in the snow and warmth entered into his soul.

The snowman melted.

It was going to be a Christmas Day full of joy. Here. Today. Where they used to live.

Autumn pushed at her eyeglasses and smiled as she tore the wrapping paper off a small package. "I know that this is not an engagement ring, Ian, because you are much too much of a romantic to wrap an ordinary package with a standard type Christmas wrapping paper and then give it to me. I mean, it is a nice thought, but Santa Claus wrapping paper is not my idea of romance." She looked up, paused on her mission of tearing off the paper, pushed at her eyeglasses again and blinked a few times.

"Right?"

Ian smiled and shrugged his shoulders. Often with Autumn, not speaking any words was the best strategy. They were sitting underneath the Christmas tree in Autumn's apartment, exchanging a few gifts with each other. Money was in short supply, especially so with Ian, but they agreed to give each other a few small items. Lionel was in on the celebration too. Right now, he was pushing a rolling ball with a jingle bell all over the apartment. The old cat was not napping. It seemed as if meeting Autumn had revitalized his life too. Ian tapped at the small box that contained the ring in his vest pocket and made sure it was still there. It was. Since it looked as if their plans to meet with Autumn's parents on Christmas Day for a joyful reunion and celebration and for Ian to give a heartfelt proposal of marriage went south with his painful discussion with Mr. Gleason, Ian turned to an alternate plan. He planned to go with Autumn for a walk in the local park after dinner, using the excuse to walk off their Christmas dinner. The park was nearby, just a short walk down the street and a left turn and a right turn. A few days earlier, he had found the perfect spot to propose to Autumn. Underneath a glorious oak tree with a twisted trunk and amazing branches. The Christmas snow would be a gentle touch.

Yet, in Ian's mind, he wondered about the Christmas Roses. . ..

"Oh, Ian. Thank you! A yarn spindle! It is lovely. Perfect. It will keep Lionel from tangling my yarn while I knit. He loves to play with my work."

Ian winked and said, "You are welcome. I love to play with your work too. Especially in removing some of those knitted lacy things that you wear . . .

underneath other things."

Autumn laughed and playfully tapped Ian on the shoulder. "You animal you! Such thoughts on Christmas Day." She then changed her voice to add some huskiness to it, "You can unwrap my best present later. I think you will enjoy my latest handwork. It has no support at all for the girls."

Ian was just about to answer when Autumn's cell phone lit up and the ringer went off. She gently set the present paper and the box aside and picked it up. Her beautiful eyes widened while she stared at the number on the screen of the phone, and she blinked and feverishly pushed at her eyeglasses.

"Autumn? Honey . . . who is it?"

"My goodness, Ian! It is my father calling." She tapped at the screen, lifted the phone to her ear and locked her eyes with her lover. Even Lionel sensed the change in the mood and he stopped pushing his bell around the apartment, walked over and jumped into Ian's lap.

"Hello. Yes, Merry Christmas, Dad," Autumn said and then quickly added, "this is quite a surprise. I mean a delightful surprise. Actually, honestly, this is an amazing surprise! Yes, Ian is here and Lionel is here too. Huh? Oh yes, Lionel is Ian's cat. I mean . . . he is kind of our cat. We share him. We knew each other in one of our past lives. Yes, I assure you that he is a cat in this life, Dad. Lately he is always here at my place. He goes everywhere with us." Autumn stopped speaking and it was then that Ian saw the tears filling up in the edges of her eyes. Ian was now unsuccessfully fighting back the tears too.

"Ah yes, please, let me check with Ian first, but I

think that we can come over for dinner. We were just having some sliced deli turkey, and we had some. . .. Ah yes, I am checking now, Dad."

Ian was waving and nodding fervently while his heart pounded in his chest.

"Yes, Ian is right here, nodding and waving as if his pants are on fire. I mean, I plan to set him on fire later, but perhaps, that is too much information to share with my father."

Autumn laughed, and Ian swore that he overheard Mr. Gleason laugh too. "Yes, cocktails at two and dinner at four. Gotcha. And yes, bring Lionel too. Of course, we will bring Lionel and his new ringy-thingy ball. He got it for Christmas. He pushes it all over the apartment and the bell rings, and honestly," Autumn stopped speaking and pushed at her eyeglasses and then continued speaking, "it is rather annoying but when we compared it to the other potential toys . . . oh yes, Dad. I love you too. Dad, I love you with all my heart and soul. And Mom, too. Of course, Mom too. Yes. See you at two. Oh yes, Ian is a very careful driver. He kind of drives like Grandpa used to drive. Goodbye, Dad. Thank you."

Autumn hit the end call button on her cell phone and slowly and gently set the phone onto the floor. Shock and awe were all over her lovely face. Lionel hopped off Ian's lap and the two of them wiggled over to Autumn. Ian draped his arms around Autumn and gently kissed her cheek while Lionel rubbed at her legs.

"He called and invited us to Christmas dinner at home. Where we used to live. He told me that he loves me, future husband. I bet the roses bloomed. I know in my heart that the roses bloomed! I used the perfect starter fertilizer and took great care of the roots when I planted them. I grew those plants from precious seeds, Ian. Precious. It is magic, Ian. Just as our love is. M-a-g-i-c."

"Please come in, for just a second. Don't remove your overcoats and hats. Please," Mr. Gleason had answered the front door to the mansion and was waving, Autumn, Ian, and Lionel, who was neatly tucked in his carrying crate into the foyer of the home. Mr. Gleason seemed quite animated, and Autumn and Ian looked at each other with puzzled looks on their faces. Mrs. Gleason stood next to Mr. Gleason and she, too, wore an overcoat, gloves and a hat.

"Please, Mr. Fall, if we might have a word. Over here. In private. Please excuse us. Ashley, it is fine. Please, I have this. We will be out and about for a few minutes and please, upon our return, we will enjoy cocktails in the sitting room."

"Yes, of course, Mr. Gleason. Thank you."

"And uncork some of our best champagne. Please, you and Harold will join us. I mean, in the sitting room. Tell Harold for me. Will you?"

"Yes . . . of course. Join you, Mr. Gleason?"

It was obvious that Ashley was flustered at his out-of-character behavior and suggestion.

"Yes, indeed. It is Christmas Day, Ashley. Christmas Day. We are celebrating . . . everything."

Mr. Gleason's voice was singsong in its tone.

Mr. Gleason nodded and waved as Ashley scooted

off with an ashen face but a slight smile on her face. Ian squeezed Autumn's hand and handed off Lionel to her. Autumn nodded and smiled as Mrs. Gleason moved closer to greet her daughter and gush over Lionel. Ian followed Mr. Gleason as he briskly walked over to the far corner of the entrance foyer and motioned for them to stand next to the huge Christmas tree tucked in the corner of the foyer. Near the staircase. Mr. Gleason reached out his hand, Ian grasped it, and the two men shook hands.

Mr. Gleason lowered his voice to just above a whisper and said, "I owe you a sincere and profound apology for my treatment of you and for my harsh and ill-used words when we met a few days ago, Mr. Fall. Please accept my sincerest apology and my deepest condolences on the loss of your parents. That type of pain is unimaginable to me. Yet, you persevere, and that is a credit to your strength and your character. Autumn is a very lucky young woman and you are a very lucky young man. I am sorry to hear of the loss of your uncle too. It is readily apparent that your parents and your aunt and uncle raised a very special young man. I need to convey strongly to you that you have my permission, and, in fact, you have Autumn's parent's blessing to ask our daughter to marry you."

"Thank you, sir, for your condolences and kind words. I accept your apology and look forward to a wonderful day. I have to ask you . . . did three very special Christmas ghosts visit you last night?"

Mr. Gleason laughed and placed his arm around Ina's shoulders. "No ghosts, Mr. Fall, or rather, Ian. No ghosts, but I do have a surprise. Or maybe it is not a surprise at all."

"The plants bloomed, right? You knew where to look for them because it is a special place. To our Autumn and to you too. Right?"

"You, Ian, are the perfect match for our daughter because I can see that you both ask too many questions. Come along and I mean this in the gentlest way, but please do not say a word."

Ian followed Mr. Gleason and the two men joined Autumn, Mrs. Gleason and Lionel. Mr. Gleason held his hand in the air and said, "Follow me. No questions! No supposition! It is Christmas, and please, I ask you to give this old man the chance to provide his family with a surprise."

Autumn went to open her mouth and Ian knew that she was going to ask if the plants bloomed and follow that question with a long technical diatribe about the science of plants, but Ian gently clamped his hand over her mouth and interrupted her before the words could arrive.

"Ah, no, my love. No questions. Do you promise?" Autumn smiled under Ian's hand, held her hand over her chest in the sign of a promise, and nodded. It was a joyful trek in the snow; Ian and Autumn were hand-in-hand with Ian using his other hand while holding Lionel in his cage, who was wide-eyed at the journey and the adventure. Mr. and Mrs. Gleason led the way, and they too held hands. It was there next to the rock that all their tears of joy fell into the snow and the pale white flowers winked at them. And the yellow centers danced in the light, and their magic enveloped their souls.

Mr. Gleason waved everyone in for a group hug

and as his voice choked over with emotions; his normally powerful and deep voice barely squeaked the words out amongst the emotions leaving his soul.

"I want to say . . . Autumn, our glorious daughter, please accept my apologies for my attitude and my bitterness, and honestly, for my foolishness. I hope you can forgive me and we can move on in love and in life. You have all of my support and my love forever. I love you, dear Autumn. Now and forever, we all love you."

Autumn buried her head into her father's chest and whispered, "Of course, I forgive you, Dad. I, too, love you. Now and forever."

Ian knew it was time, and he actually preferred Autumn's parents, and of course Lionel, to witness this. He plucked the box out of his vest pocket, held Autumn's hands, and then dropped down to one knee in the snow while everyone gasped and Autumn jumped up and down in joy. It was one wave of emotion after another!

For once, Autumn could not speak. . ..

"Autumn Lynne Gleason, will you marry me? I want nothing more to be your husband and no longer be your future husband. Please, Autumn . . . marry me. Please."

Autumn nodded her head fervently and after some tears and an atypical pause, the words finally arrived, "Yes, I will marry you. Of course, my answer is yes!"

When Ian removed the ring from the box and gently placed it upon her finger, it seemed as if more of the plants bloomed as her tears fell into the snow. Then again, that is how the legend went.

Tears, blooms, joy, and love. Where we used to live. Where everyone will always live. Home.

"Please tell me more about this business of opening up your own delicatessen, Ian." Mr. Gleason requested as the two men sat in the same brown leather chairs in Mr. Gleason's office that they sat in a few days earlier. The two men nursed two glasses of Jameson Irish whiskey. Their bellies were full, and life was great. Lionel was sleeping in the remaining chair, napping away the rest of the waning afternoon of Christmas Day. Lionel had enjoyed some turkey, too. The old cat now owned that chair too, but Mr. Gleason seemed not to mind at all. He actually enjoyed the old cat's company.

"Well, Mr. Gleason. . .."

Mr. Gleason interrupted Ian and said, "Please, call me, Dad."

Ian nodded and restarted, "Okay. Dad, I have a vision. A typical city delicatessen with all the usual offerings, with a twist to our heritage. Some Irish, Scottish, English goods and food. Maybe, homemade meat pies, steak and kidney, mutton, mince pies, bean pies. Some shepherd's pie and my partner at the deli now, Susan, well, she makes homemade soups that are simply amazing. I was thinking of a location outside of the city of Paterson. Maybe up on Belmont Avenue in Haledon Borough or over on Union Boulevard in Totowa Borough."

Ian studied Mr. Gleason's eyes for a reaction. The old attorney swirled the whiskey glass around in the air, and the golden liquid swirled and licked the edges of the glass.

"I like it, Ian. I like it a lot. You will need to do a traffic study for the locations. I have some connections to assist with that."

Ian nodded and mouthed a "thank you" while taking a sip of the whiskey.

"I might be persuaded to invest in this venture with the proper business plan. Can you write that for me, Ian? After the holidays."

"That would be wonderful, Dad. Amazing. Of course, I will write it. Thank you for the consideration."

"Do you have a name selected for the business?"

Ian smiled and without hesitation, the answer jumped from his lips, "Autumn's Place."

"Yes, perfect. I love it. Love it. Say, after the holidays, I am making a phone call to an old connection over in the city. He is on the board of directors for one of the large botanical gardens over there. I hear that he has an opening for a master horticulturist and I might just put a word in for a lovely young woman that we both love dearly. It is also a lovely place to hold a wedding ceremony."

Mr. Gleason nodded, smiled, and leaned back in his chair. He picked up the glass, downed the rest of the whiskey, and pointed at Ian as if to request that he do the same.

"I need to say to you, Ian, that I do have a special request."

"Sir?"

"Next Christmas and many Christmas Days afterwards, I want little Ian or little Autumn and other little tykes running around here. All over the place. Screaming, yelling, and tearing the place all apart. Chasing Lionel into every corner of the house, and Ian, there are many corners in this house. I want to buy the grandchildren all kinds of gifts and spoil your children rotten. I want to hold their little hands, lead them out to the corner of this property, and show them some very magical plants. I want them to sit on that large rock and tell me their dreams and wishes. Besides, I am sure that you will enjoy the assignment of fulfilling my request."

Ian laughed and added, "I will do my best, Dad. I think we can work on that."

Mr. Gleason stood up, and Ian handed him his empty glass. "Good. Thank you. You need to get busy working on that. Christmas has a funny way of creeping up on you rather quickly. After all, someone has to learn the delicatessen business."

"How about a future lawyer? You know, to perpetuate the heritage, Dad."

Mr. Gleason smiled. He grew pensive for a few seconds then shook his head and added, "Only if they want to, Ian. Only if that is where their heart leads them."

Mr. Gleason took a few steps, stopped, and he winked and said, "Refill time, Ian. Refill time. I know a very brilliant young man who once told me that what matters the most is whom we loved, how we loved, and how we touched each other. When it is all over for us in this world, love is what Christmas and life are really all about. I intend to live the rest of my life that way, Ian. In the meantime, the day is still young. Let us share another drink or two, go find our lovely women and celebrate this Christmas Day and all the joy it brings to us. Together. All together. Today and forever."

Out on the far edges of the property on the estate of the Gleason family, the edges of darkness crept in on the plants nestled in the snow near the large rock on the edges of the woods. Darkness and shadows crept across the glistening snow as the sun slowly faded and another Christmas Day began to end. The wind blew hard and some dry powdery snow shook free from the limbs of the trees towering high above the now sleeping Christmas Roses. The snow landed on the blooms in gentle waves, the snowflakes clung onto the flower petals and the green leaves of the plants as if they were diamonds sent from Heaven.

Perhaps they were.

THE END

Flash Eighteen

The Strange Patterns of the Sky

The blacksmith did his best when he pounded it out and then dipped it in oil. He did not have the most elaborate set-up. Just a small shop on the edge of his garage and within the confines thereof.

It was a part-time gig for him. He worked at it on Saturdays. In Sussex County, New Jersey.

It brought in a few extra dollars and helped him to unwind on the weekends from his full-time job. His father taught him the ins and outs of the trade. Every extra dollar helped. These days and then some too.

It was a glorious rooster. Most weathervanes are. Oil-treated. His wife could smell the oil-laden smoke in his work clothes for days.

The smith's wife sold the weathervane at a stand at the farmer's market on the following Saturday. Eighty-five dollars. A nice sale it was.

Indeed.

The weather on Christmas Day was precarious. The weathervane did not know which way to point. It was a very good thing that the bearings were sound and tight and they could keep up with the wind.

Swirling winds and strange patterns in the sky. Clouds on the move. A rush towards the unknown.

It had snowed a few days earlier and now it was clear and cold. As the day chugged on, the weather turned blustery and the temperature grew colder and colder toward the afternoon.

The wind first changed to the west . . . then off to the east. The weathervane spun and kept up with the winds.

It was a glorious display of weathervane prowess.

The wind picked up, and the weather changed once more. Now it was a north wind, and the temperature plummeted. Clouds rolled in and snow spit out of the sky.

Their love prevailed, and the weathervane spun in a vain (vane) effort to keep up with the changes.

They kissed near the flowers of the Christmas Rose. Near where the weathervane pointed the direction of the wind and the sky.

They kissed while standing ankle-deep in the snow. Kisses in the snow on Christmas Day are extra special. Snow was simply a bonus.

They kissed with dreams in their hearts and in their heads.

Young lovers often do that. It is only age, experience, and life that taints those kisses.

On the top peak of the roof of the out-building, the weathervane spun rather furiously. The sky signaled change. A hint of blue, but it was mostly grey with touches of reflected sunlight that glowed with reds and yellows.

The patterns of the sky are so unpredictable and so is the temperature at this time of year. The temperature dropped rapidly as the weather front moved into the area.

Some flickers and licks of snow chased in the wind around the weathervane as the day waned.

Their love would remain intact forever.

As did the weathervane point, so did the wind.

The bearings were sound and tight. Eighty-five dollars so well spent.

It was a grand and glorious display of weathervane abilities because the patterns of the sky were so unpredictable.

As were the clouds and the wind.

On Christmas Day and thereafter.

Flash Nineteen

The Drill Instructor

"Mens! I will tell you here and now that some of you standing here right now, will die! Yes, you will die! No sense in sugarcoating shit. Because, guess what? It will still be shit. No, I am not God, so I cannot tell you when or how, some of you will die, but I know this to be true. In my twenty or so years of teaching and training patsy-asses like all of you losers are right now, to become Marines, I have learned from experience that Marines die. Some of you might die in combat, with a bullet clean through your head. A clean kill contains elements of honor when you are in battle. Others might tumble on your sorry asses, and be run over by a truck and have all your guts pushed outta of ya! Others will succumb to some rare-ass disease, but what you have to understand is that you will die in service to your beloved Marine Corps and to your country. To die as a warrior, as a United States Marine, is an honor. It is not as if you are dying, no, no no, Mens, it is as if you are promoted to a higher mission!"

While he bellowed at the top of his voice, the drill instructor slowly walked back and forth in front of his new recruits. It was the first few hours of the critical first meeting, the first day of basic training. His highly polished shoes glistened in the sun, his uniform, despite the heat, remained crisp and fresh. If you looked closely, you could see hints of beads of sweat working their way down the sides of his temples.

Despite the popular opinion of the multitudes, drill instructors are human. They do sweat. However, the drops of sweat contain salt, honor, and courage.

The drill instructor stopped pacing and with one arm, and his hand outstretched to Heaven, he dramatically pointed in the air to the American flag waving on the pole high above his head.

His previously bellowing voice softened and lowered. The drill instructor grew solemn.

It almost seemed impossible for him to do so, but he did lower his booming voice as he explained, "For that flag, to wave in the breeze, above our heads, and for it to fly as freely as it does, unencumbered, proud, strong, it took a damn lot of blood and guts. Mens, the expectations of those who shed their blood and their guts, is that there would be many to follow in their footsteps. You will not let them down, nor let your beloved United States Marine Corps down, your country down, or God down. I know in my heart that is true, so help me God."

The drill instructor turned and faced the front and center of the formation of want-to-be-Marines, he stood tall and proud in front of the nervous recruits, he tucked his arms at his side and his face was stoic, yet proud. He lowered his head so that you could just see the top of his eyes ominously peering out from under the edge of his drill instructor's hat.

Once again, he spoke in a somber tone, "Mens, be forewarned . . . I know in my heart that this is true and if I fail in my mission, if I fail that flag, fail my beloved Marine Corps and fail those who have shed their blood and their guts . . . then, I will gladly pay the price of having done so."

Flash Twenty

Spinning

An old hockey goaltender from the past hockey games of long ago suddenly arrived in his life. It was time to stop dreaming and pretending. The old goalie whispered reality to him through the ancient goalie mask that he wore.

It was a surprise. In more ways than one.

A vastly understated surprise.

Such is life.

Such was his life.

Superheroes did not exist, although many persons told him that he was a real superhero.

It was not true. If he only stopped spinning through his perceived glorious life then, he would realize that he was actually a fool.

This damn fool had worked hard for everything. He worked endlessly. Day-by-day. Hour-by-hour. Endlessly, with the mission always in his mind. Tapping away at his keyboard. Word-by-word. Letter-to-letter.

Endlessly.

Other people abused him and they all used him for what he was good to them for, laughed at him, and took advantage of him, yet he plodded onward. Through a maze of words and madness.

A damn fool.

He travelled millions of miles, on the ground, in the air, by rail, by foot, and by car. In his mind and in his heart. He never stopped.

For him, for the people he loved, for his family, he worked until he collapsed in his bed and at the end of his spirit. His spirit finally gave out and gave up the cause.

Yet, in his defense, he never stopped working until the end. When the end came and the truth unfolded before his eyes, he ran out into the cold air and stood still. He looked up at the sky, began to spin around as he kept his feet firmly planted on the ground and he decided that he should hold his arms stretched out just as far as his arms allowed him to do so. He spun around and around until he became too dizzy to continue. The sky never looked so amazing. His last thought before he gave up and died was how much he loved her, his family, and this world.

Then he stopped spinning.

So did the words. Very few people ever really supported him in his endless quest to find the correct words to plug into the pages in just the right spot, nor did they read them, or encourage him to write onward. Only a handful. He could count them using the fingers on one hand.

Yet he did write onward—until the spinning finally ended.

An old hockey goaltender from the past hockey games of long ago suddenly arrived while he drifted off to the life-after. No more would he dream or pretend. The old goalie whispered the reality of Heaven to him through the old goalie mask that he wore. It sounded as if was a choir of angels singing to him. He realized that it was.

It was a surprise. In more ways than one.

A vastly understated surprise.

Such is life.

Such was his life and the end of it.

So were all the words. They were a surprise. All of them. Every single one. In death and in sweet relief, he hoped that someone read them. Every single one.

Reboot One *

"Laziness. Lazy bums. We have the same trouble in the shop where I work. It is a shame. The problem with this country today, is that, everyone wants to jump in the back of the wagon and make a few poor slobs pull it. Free rides. It all goes along fine until a hill comes along. Then some freeloaders got to climb out, get off their lazy asses and push. That's when the trouble starts."

*A tip of the cold beer mug to the old man, courtesy of "Christmas Cocktails. Mistletoe and Mayhem."

Spark Seven

Bossy

"Clocks, watches, and other timepieces all can be rather bossy. Always telling us what time it is. Never relenting. Even for a second."

Spark Eight

Reality

"We move from the far right to the far left. Eventually, we land in the dead center because that is where the reality is."

Spark Nine

Look Around

"Look both ways before you cross the street. Also, look up and down because you really do not know if aliens are real or not and a spaceship might just decide to fly in and land on you."

Spark Ten

Hold Hands with a Stranger

"Grab that stranger's hand and love them forever because you never know when you might cross paths with them again, both now and forever. Words and kindness mean everything, so never underestimate them."

Spark Eleven

Words

"Give me dusty books with a musty smell as I open and turn the pages, some thoughtful and powerful words, the love of God, a colorful and glorious sunset, and a smooth Irish whiskey and I do not need anything else in this life because I am a rich man."

Spark Twelve

Back-up

"The back-up quarterback on the football team is always everyone's favorite player."

Spark Thirteen

Perception

"Who are you to judge me? You have never walked alongside of me for a second of my life, nor a minute, or an hour, or a day. Until you do so, then I can assure you that your perception is not my reality."

Spark Fourteen

In the Quietest of Moments

"In the quietest of moments of my life; when the dark is all around me and the stillness weighs heavy, that is when I am able to hear the loudest and the clearest voices in my mind."

Spark Fifteen

The Ego Induced Bravado
Humankind's Greatest Sin

"There comes a time when every student think that they know more than the teacher does."

Spark Sixteen

My Fiction Writing Rules

"When you read my fiction writings, believe only half of what I wrote to be nonfiction, then divide that material into quarters and one-half-of-what remains is true."

Spark Plus Seventeen

A Quiz on Random Jethro Tull Appearances

"In the middle of July, if the progressive rock band, Jethro Tull led by Ian Anderson MBE randomly shows up on your front lawn of your home in Florida at seven o'clock in the morning and begins to play *Locomotive Breath*, you should:

A: Immediately put the house up for sale and move to Alaska. It is too cold in Alaska, even in July, for Jethro Tull to perform on your front lawn. Besides, it is too damn hot in Florida, anyway.

B: Run out of the house and ask Ian if you can film the performance on your smartphone and put the video on the internet because no one would believe that this was actually occurring. Mr. Anderson seldom allows unauthorized filming of his performances, even if this is your own front lawn, so please do not be disappointed if he says no.

C: Stop being so damn cheap and upgrade to a better quality of Scotch whiskey that does not cause hallucinatory behavior.

D: Stop eating spicy food before bedtime.

E: Forget about the entire incident, let the band spot a few tunes, put a coin box on a folding table in the yard to make a few bucks, turn the air conditioning thermostat down to 66 degrees and go back to bed.

F: Ask Mr. Anderson, if he still has those skin-tight pants and high fringe leather boots that he wore in 1978, and if he does, if you could borrow them, put them on and strut around the yard as if you are a drunken rooster while they perform. Only do this if you are confident that you look really, really, really, good in skin-tight pants and high-fringe leather boots. Otherwise, the police will arrive and arrest you.

G: All of the above."

Flash Twenty-One

The Old Apple Tree and the Young Boy with the Limp

Children can be so cruel to one another.

"It happens. Disease damages. It is no one's fault. His right leg will always be a little shorter than his left leg is."

The baby's parents stared in at the doctor with intense concern upon their faces. The doctor sensed the concern, and he performed a quick layer of damage control with his ensuing words to relieve their concerns.

"Look," the good doctor said with an air of sympathy within his voice, "he will never be a sprinting champion, or a soccer star, or an athlete of any kind, but aside from his limp, with some intense rehabilitation work, I am quite sure that he will lead a normal life. Maybe, even, do extraordinary things."

The father looked up at the doctor with a deep sadness in his eyes. Often, deep stares from human eyes are so telling in their meaning.

"Thank you, doctor. Ah, rehabilitation? We are simple farmers. We own several apple orchards. Money is tight. To say the least. It always will be. Nothing much changes when you are a farmer. Yet, our trees have stories to tell, and to hear, and much love to give. Please, tell me, how much does intense rehabilitation cost?"

The doctor sighed.

"Ha, ha, ha! Old short leg has no friends! All he has is his stupid books. He always walks around with his head down and his eyes glued to the pages of stupid books," the evil bully said to the young boy with the limp as a squeeze of disgusting foamy spittle edged out of the corners of his mouth. Bullies are ugly in so many ways. If their mothers could only see them now.

"I have friends! More friends than you do," the young boy with the limp, protested his response to the bully.

"You do? Who? Crusoe, Scrooge, Holmes and Watson? Dickens? Ha! Characters in your dusty old books do not count as actual friends."

The young boy with the limp hung his head and sadly walked away with his books tucked under his arm.

"We will need to level the north quadrant come the spring of next year," the farmer said to his helper as they shared a few beers together on a cold winter's night and planned the farming for the next year. "As soon as the snow melts, we will pull 'em out, cut 'em down and sell the apple wood. They are under producers. Especially the big, old one in the first row. Only a few quality fruits last year. Shame, cuz, used it to be a helluva tree. Just too old now, I 'magine. Disease must'a damaged it now."

The helper nodded. He made a note in his pad and took a sip of beer when he finished scribbling with his pencil.

When you are a farmer, the winter was for

planning.

Hearing the words, the young boy with the limp picked his head out of the book he was reading and he carefully listened to his father's words.

A single tear ran down his cheek. He loved the pinks and whites of apple blossoms in the spring.

Disease damaged it.

It was bitterly cold. January can tear at you and chill at you and bite at you as none other of the twelve months can.

Undaunted from the bite of the cold, the young boy with the limp walked through the crusty snow. He stopped in front of the old tree, and he studied it. The big old one in the first row. The young boy with the limp knew that tree was the leader for the rest of the trees. He could feel it because the young boy with the limp could do extraordinary things.

The twisty branches reached toward Heaven and beyond. They were dormant in the cold and sleeping until the warmth awoke them. Yet, the young boy with the limp knew that they could hear his words and feel his love.

Love can warm the coldest day, dispel the harshest wind and echo all the way to Heaven.

He sat down in the snow at the base of the tree and opened his book.

The first words that he read from the first dusty, old book were loud and clear, "I think that I shall never see. A poem as lovely as a tree. A tree whose. . .."

Every day, the young boy with the limp arrived, and every day, he read his books aloud at the base of the big, old apple tree that was the first in the row.

Adventures of Holmes, the healed bitterness of Scrooge and the trickery of the dodger.

The young boy with the limp had many friends.

Spring arrived, and the snow melted. Rebirth of the previous latent and interesting dormancy arrived too. Warmth and sun, and birds and soft breezes that caused the snow to run away into the edges of the orchard.

"Well, faint be my heart," the farmer said as he gazed at the extraordinary display of stunning apple blossoms perched on countless twisty branches framed in a clear blue sky. Branches that reached to Heaven and beyond. Pinks and white and gentle pistils waved to the old farmer in the lovely spring breeze. Welcoming his gaze, loving his thoughts and embracing his care. It took his breath away.

"Fooled me. I guess that old tree recovered and lookie at that. So did the rest of the trees in the row, too. Gonna be an exceptional year."

The farmer's helper nodded and scribbled in his notepad as he crossed off his notes from last winter.

The glorious apple trees in the old apple orchard had stories to tell, and to hear, and much love to give.

As did the young boy with the limp.

As do we all.

ABOUT THE AUTHOR

Way back in time, when the dinosaurs first died off, at the ripe old age of sixteen, Paul John Hausleben wrote three stories for a creative writing class in high school. Enrolled in a vocational school, and immersed in trade courses and apprenticeship, left little time for writing ventures, but PJH wrote three exceptional and entertaining stories. Paul John Hausleben's stories caught the eye of two English teachers in the college-preparatory academic programs, and they pulled the author out of his basic courses and plopped him in advanced English and writing courses. One of the English teachers had immense faith in Paul's talents, and she took PJH's stories, helped him brush them up, and submitted them to a periodical for publication. To PJH's astonishment, the periodical published all three of the stories and sent him a royalty check for fifty dollars and . . . that was it. PJH did not write anymore because life got in his way. Fast forward to 2009 and while living on the road in Atlanta, Georgia (and struggling to communicate with the locals who did not speak New Jersey) for his full-time job, PJH took a part-time job writing music reviews for a progressive rock website, and that gig caused the writing bug to bite PJH once more. He recalled those old stories and found the old manuscripts hiding in a dusty box. After some doodling around with them, PJH decided to revisit them. Two stories became the nucleus for the anthology now known as *The Time Bomb in The Cupboard and Other Adventures of Harry and Paul.* The other story became the anchor story for collection known as, *The Christmas Tree and Other Christmas Stories, Tales for a Christmas Evening.* Now, many years and over thirty-five published works later, along with countless blogs and other work, PJH continues to write. Where and when it stops, only the author really knows.

On the other hand, does he really know?

If you ask Paul John Hausleben, he will tell you that he is not an author, he is just a storyteller. His mission is to continue to write and tell stories to warm your heart, make you laugh, and sometimes make you cry, just a little. Most of all, he deals in memories, and helps you to remember the good times of your own life, and the special people who touched you along the way. Paul was born and raised in Paterson, and then nearby Haledon, New Jersey, and began writing at an early age. He revisited a writing career later in his life, and he now is the author of a number of novels, compilations, short stories and audio and video works. Most of his work touches upon nostalgic remembrances of simpler times, and tells the stories of heartfelt, humorous, and special human relationships. Other than writing, among many careers both paid and unpaid, he is a former semi-professional hockey goaltender, a former military radio operator, a music fan and music reviewer, an avid sports fan, photographer and amateur radio operator. He now resides in Somewhere, U.S.A., but his heart always remains along Belmont Avenue in good old Paterson, and Haledon, New Jersey.

Paul John Hausleben

Somewhat of a Correct Answer

G: All of the above

Other Work by Mr. Paul John Hausleben

The Time Bomb in The Cupboard and Other
Adventures of Harry and Paul

The Night Always Comes, Another story from the
Adventures of Harry and Paul

Reunion, A sequel to the Night Always Comes and
Another story from the Adventures of Harry and
Paul

The Miracle Tree, Another story from the
Adventures of Harry and Paul

The Chronicles of Henson

Heaven's Gain
The Final Adventure of Harry and Paul

Geyer Street Gardens
Beneath the Mask of a Hockey Goaltender
Another story from the Adventures of Harry and
Paul

Where the River Bends and Curls

Tales of the Quiet Stranger in the Black Hat

Paul John Hausleben

Crows on a High Wire

Flying

Christmas Cocktails

Pastor Henson's Garden

The Summer Collection

And a few others too!

You may write to the author at ctte27@gmail.com

Published by God Bless the Keg Publishing LLC

Henrico, Virginia, U.S.A.

You may write to the publisher at
Godblessthekegpublishing@gmail.com

"Life's simple pleasures are so often the best ones!"

Follow God Bless the Keg Publishing LLC and Paul John Hausleben on Facebook and enjoy samples of his photography, general tidbits of interest, receive updates on new releases, and enjoy his general meanderings.

Paul John Hausleben

Made in United States
North Haven, CT
31 March 2023

34782814R00171